The Case of the Lost Antrum

Rhiannon D. Elton

The Case of the Lost Antrum © Rhiannon D. Elton 2022
The Wolflock Cases: Book 9
Second edition

ISBN: 978-0-6487636-8-0 (paperback)

First Edition published August 2017
Second Edition published March 2022

info@rhiannoneltonauthor.com

Cover compiled by Rhiannon D. Elton

Cataloguing-in-Publication information for this title is listed with the National Library of Australia.

Published in Australia by Rhiannon D. Elton and Pelaia Adventures

This project is supported by the Regional Arts Development Fund (RADF). RADF is a partnership between the Queensland Government and Logan City Council to support arts and culture in regional Queensland.

Dedicated to Stewart,
Heroes take action and because you believed in me, I
took action. Thank you for your unwavering support
and friendship.

Get More of the Magic & Mystery...

subscribe.rhiannoneltonauthor.com/more

If you want more clues, more magic and more mystery, let me know by going to the Wolflock Cases subscribe page.

You'll get clues, maps, sketches, behind the scenes stories, lore and much more! You'll also be the first to know when a new story is coming out so you can solve the mystery before your friends.

If you sign up with the magical link below, you'll also get a free downloadable map to follow Wolflock's journey to Mystentine University.

subscribe.rhiannoneltonauthor.com/more

Declaration of Intention

Merry meet,

The purpose of the books the author writes is to give representation to as many peoples, creatures and landscapes as they can. Although written from the perspective of a Caucasian teenage boy, the author hopes to offer a light into the harmony of different cultures and creeds of people. The author's aim is to promote harmony, understanding and compassion in all areas, while also inspiring readers to stand up against injustice and be critical thinkers in life.

While the author does their best to research, interview and highlight the best parts of people, they are only human and can make mistakes. The author asks you gently educate them by sending them an email in order to discuss anything that may have caused harm to a group of people unintentionally.

The author believes that the cure for ignorance is education, but please approach the topic cordially in order to avoid any knee-jerk cognitive dissonance.

Finally, the viewpoints displayed in the books comes from a particular character and is not necessarily that of the author's. The author seeks to display flaws, growth and human nature on many levels, and hopes that you will analyse the character of the protagonist without adopting any negative behaviours from them.

Merry part, and merry meet again.

Rhiannon Op Eltron

MYSTENTINE INNER CITY MAP

RAVEN'S BURROW
MOUNTAIN GUIDES

MYSTENTINE GUARD
HEADQUARTERS

DR VAXTADLARES
APOTHECARY

MS INGI'RS
TOWNHOUSE

LEIPURES PASTRIES

395 WAREHOUSES
& STORAGE

MR & MRS DALURS
MANOR

CHAPTER 1

The City of Magic

The dark starry sky above rose like a curtain on a stage, unveiling the monumental mountain before them. The great mountain wrapped itself around the city with two rings of twenty-foot-high stone walls encapsulating it against a background of powdery blue, skirted by fluffy lavender clouds. It looked like a giant mother softly holding the city.

The gentle clatter of the carriage and Khra's enormous hooves clopping against the paved roads were the only noise they heard. The outer suburbs beyond the second wall wove together like a twisted fishing net interspersed with small farms. Chimney stacks started to send streams of smoke into the air and the smell of woodsmoke and baking roused the houses. Unusually coloured lights winked in the windows as they rode past; oil lamps, balls of magical light, and different science contraptions that glowed as the people readied for their day.

They approached the first wall of the city. The Guards keeping watch stepped forward, looking dubiously at the horse.

"Uh... Merry meet. Name and business in town?"

Wolflock opened the door and stepped out, grateful for being able to stretch his legs. "Ah. Merry meet, Guardsman. I am Mr Wolflock Felen. This is my travelling companion Mr Mothy Enitnelav and we're on our way to the university. My friend here is going to be getting hungry soon, would you be able to recommend a good breakfast eatery?" He patted Khra's side as he moved towards the gate.

Crafted from gigantic trees and carved iron brackets, each piece of the gate was engraved with landscapes of historically significant moments for the city and warding sigils. He wondered what the sigils were for or if they were even still active.

"I see. Continue down the main road to the inner

gate. I'm not familiar with the food in the inner city."

"Oh, you have to go to Leipuri's Pastries. You'll smell them before you see them. They make the best breakfast," said the second guard as the first circled the carriage.

"Excellent. Is there a stable on the inner wall? Our horse has delicate skin and I'd rather keep her out of the sun."

"Best get a blanket on her now then, it's a good hour to the inner city." The first guard picked his teeth.

"Even on the main road?"

"Oh, aye. Weekday traffic is never good unless you can weave through the backroads. This carriage ain't making it through those pokey streets," said the first guard as he finished his lap around the carriage.

Khra snorted and looked back at Wolflock with her big dark eyes.

"Let's find a stable for you here, then. Mothy and I will get a hansom for the rest of the trip. Anyone you could suggest for us, gentlemen?"

Khra bobbed her head up and down in agreement.

"You'll be wanting the noblest of steeds. There's only one who's ever awake at this hour," the first guard snorted.

"Ah yes," said the second as if they knew

something Wolflock didn't. "The great Sir Hedginton the sixteenth. Go through the gate here and it's your first left. You'll find your noble steed there. Your horse can stable for the day as well."

Wolflock nodded and thanked the men before stepping up onto Khra's driver's seat. Fully awake now, he wanted the best view of the city. The driver's seat offered him height and complete visual freedom. Mothy stayed in the carriage.

The guards stepped to the side of the gate and turned pumpkin sized blue gemstones with handles carved into their surfaces. From the stones, electric blue light zapped around the giant doors and pulled them open. With a great groaning and creaking, the middle ring of Mystentine City opened to them.

Khra started up again, trotting forward on the beautiful road. The guardsmen nodded and waited for them to pass through before talking about whether to close the gates or not again.

"It's close enough to morning, aye?" one grumbled, not wanting to put the effort into closing it now just to open it when the traffic grew.

Wolflock smiled excitedly as he looked on either side of the main road. Dimming fairy dust streetlights and trees punctuated the raised sidewalk. Each pole held a beautifully designed lantern with different coloured fairy dust piling at the bottom, with individual paintings decorating their posts, plants twisting around them, and etched with stone sculptures and gemstones that reflected the businesses that they stood sentinel for. Unlike Plugh, nothing in Mystentine looked uniform. Wolflock recalled in his hometown that the perfectly manicured streets were filled with symbolic trees and hedges, preened to an inch of their natural lives, but each forced to look exactly like the ones before. He hated it.

No two trees or shrubs growing along the Mystentine streets looked alike. They passed an old craggy tree with a crotchety trunk bent in directions perfect for climbing, with pointy leaves jutting out like little daggers. One of the shrubs held no leaves, but its grey twigs held elongated berries that looked like sapphires. Another tree had sparse brown leaves as big as his hand, with large pink flowers, but, as they drew closer, the tree hummed and the flowers flew off with little glowing pixies riding them like long handled vehicles.

The shops were even more fascinating than the trees. Wolflock saw a myriad of strange collections and services available. Gilaford's Brownie Cleaners had two doors, one for regular sized humans and one at half the height, with a window filled with antique cleaning supplies. *Gensuis Artefact Translations* had strange brass and bronze items behind the glass, as well as unrolled old scrolls and an ancient tome opened to a page displaying a mosaic picture of a dragon Wolflock could have sworn moved. Even the local grocer on the corner across from them had strange meats and vegetables Wolflock had never seen before, even with his extensive reading.

As they passed *Herberta's Hosiery and Undergarment Repairs*, Wolflock caught a glimpse at Mothy in the reflection of the large glass windows. His friend had sat himself up very straight and was giving a posh wave to the imaginary street crowds by turning his wrist. He saw Wolflock snickering at him and turned his nose up, his expression filled with mock snobbery.

Khra reached the stables after their short ride from the gate and pawed the ground. Wolflock jumped off the carriage and patted her flank.

"You go and park the carriage and find a spot to get out of the sun. I'll go and let the attendant know you're here."

She snorted in appreciation and drew the carriage into the large gap in the fence with a confused looking Mothy still inside. Wolflock grinned to himself as he hopped up the stairs.

They were finally here. They had made it. And

they had a whole quarter moon before the pass would be snowed in. The sky was clear, and nothing could dampen his spirits now that he was in the city walls. He decided, as he swaggered into the reception area of Drebbog's Pretty Ponies and Other Transports, that he'd make a point of writing to his sister to gloat.

The reception area smelled of pine ash and homely smoke, and he saw that the fireplace by the waiting area had burned down into red embers, making a soft crinkling sound. No one stood behind the reception desk. The old dark wood desk had been used frequently and for decades, as was evident by the pristine lacquer around the sides with chipped, worn patches across the top; the decorative table runner with a cartwheel pattern couldn't hide it any more than the items cluttering the desk. A large book open to yesterday's date sat with a log of all the horses and other transporting creatures coming in, going out, as well as how much they were paid, and the commission given to the stable company.

On top of the book sat a beautiful, dark wood sign with gold lettering engraved into it. Wolflock expected it to be in Shirth, which it was, but, as he looked at it to decipher it, the letters morphed into Nördlicherwald.

For all inquiries out of hours, please tell the pen your details and leave payment in the box.

Wolflock glanced at a small moneybox on the left, sitting next to a large snow eagle feather quill. He took the sign off the register book and turned it to face him, picking up the pen with his left hand. To his surprise, it jerked itself free of his grasp and hovered over the ink pot.

"Oh? Oh, I see. Umm... Wolflock-wait. Sorry." The feather flicked the page to today's date and dipped its tip in the black ink. Wolflock realised what details it wanted after he'd started speaking. "Our driver is Khra of Veildenn Deild. Staying one day. Special request, no sunlight and preferably a freshly slaughtered predatory creature for meals if a trough of blood cannot be provided."

The quill paused as if in thought, but Wolflock had made out stranger requests on the page prior and expected bookings for today.

... Non-iron stall, fresh milk and honey.

Only Marigolds, pigeon stall. Fresh venison.

Do not stall near unseelie steeds...

He didn't think those were too out of the ordinary, but one even said, "*private stall. No native Grothien speakers*", which he thought was very odd and a tad offensive. As well as, "*Needs fresh seal or blubber every three hours.*"

Those requests didn't make him feel like his was out of the ordinary at all. The pen wrote down his words, then waited. He looked at the titles on the top of the page and read the word "purpose".

"Ah... Aiding travellers. I believe she'll not have any passengers returning home."

The quill scribbled down the words, "long distance passenger transport", and then wrote, "nine sentus". At the bottom of the page under the payment column was an asterixed note that read, "If unable or unwilling to pay agreed amount, please discuss with management within business hours". Wolflock didn't think Khra had any money in her carriage, and he knew she wouldn't be able to negotiate with the manager during daylight hours, so he drew out his coin purse and placed nine small wooden coins with King Rayin's face printed into them on the book.

The quill circled the box to the left of the desk and Wolflock scooped up the coins and put them inside. He heard them fall into the counter.

The box is an anti-theft device. He thought. If anyone came in and just took it, they would grab a plain wooden box because all the money went right through it. Clever.

As he paid, the quill laid back down and fell still

once more. As he gave one more glance around the warm room, he saw the sign on the desk now read, "*Thank you and Merry Meet Again*". He left the way he came in and saw the sun now split the horizon with a golden slice, melting away the last of the dark night sky. A few people emerged from their homes and started their days. Some carried baskets of dried flowers, others rushed by with paperwork in their arms. A few boys rolled posters onto the brick fence of the stables, advertising *A concert of the century: Geraldiin Constarta playing her illustrious voce'angelii.* If it weren't booked for the Winter Solstice, he would have loved to go.

Wolflock made his way into the stable yard and found Khra's carriage parked in one of the larger places between stone marked lines. He noticed sigils carved into them.

Probably anti-theft and things like that, he pondered as he made his way to the large warehouse behind them that was the stables. A small branch of buggies and local hansom cabs had open stables where the day-to-day transport rested. He saw several sturdy horses of brown and white, and one black and white, as well as four ponies. In the rising sun, he could have sworn one of them looked like it had wings of glass that glinted rainbow colours just out of sight.

Wolflock walked into the warehouse stables and found Mothy leaning on Khra's stall as she hung her head over the railing, receiving ear scritches from him as he chatted to her.

"I've fixed the bill, so hopefully you'll be fed what you need, and you can be on your way this evening."

She blinked her big eyes at him slowly, sighing. "Thank you. You have done me... another kindness."

"Don't think on it. I didn't want you to be used for any nefarious means in order to pay back your debt. All I ask is that you work only for the Hunter's Guild from here on out. No more transporting ruffians and criminals, yes?"

She bobbed her head affirmatively. "I will harm none... unless they mean ill to my guild... and my friends." Wolflock smiled and she tousled his hair with her flexible lips. "If you are ever in need... write to the guild. I will find you. I will help."

"Merry part, Khra." Mothy touched his forehead and flicked his fingers to the horse. "And look after old Retta. We have secrets, me and her."

"Her and I," Wolflock corrected.

"Merry part, my friends," she nickered in a laugh.

"And merry meet again." And, with that, the boys said goodbye to their dark horse.

They walked out into the carriage yard and Mothy stretched his arms far above his head, bending forwards and backwards to work out his spine.

"So, do you want to walk to the inner city and explore along the way? I'm getting hungry."

"We should get a small hansom to ride with. That way we won't get lost."

"Not a large pretty?" Mothy chuckled at his own joke.

"I want to make sure we know how to get up the mountain in time." Wolflock observed the sleepy horses standing in their stalls. One of the stalls had a huge mound of white fur rising and falling as it breathed, and another had puffs of smoke drifting out of it.

"We need to stop for food along the way though. I have should have enough sentus to get six more meals, two nights lodging and a bit of help up the mountain." Mothy rolled his coin purse in his fingers, counting the coins. "... maybe one night lodging. How do you feel about checking out the temples for a night?"

Wolflock frowned at his friend, looking him up and down. He didn't feel pity, but Mothy's thriftiness made him uncomfortable. "I'll pay for our transport and lodging. You enjoy your food as you want to. We won't go without shelter or niceties. Nor will we travel with any degree of danger up the mountain through want of a guide. If you have any issue with paying, speak up and I'll cover it."

Mothy's cheeks flushed. "I can't let you do that, Wolflock."

"Nonsense. I won't go without you, and I certainly won't be sleeping on a floor in a temple. Now, which of these horses look like they know the city..." he asked the question rhetorically.

He scrutinised their sleeping faces. Some were made for speed, lean and light. Others were for carting substantial amounts of stock or luggage. To take Mothy's mind off money, he wanted one that would be bright and not too fast. They wanted to see the city, not just race through it. They had three days before they had to attempt getting up the mountain.

A clatter came from one of the gates and a short horse dramatically flicked its door open and rhythmically stepped out.

"W-w-welcome, gentlemen," he whinnied, rolling his chestnut head in a comparable way to Mothy's earlier stretch. "Sir Theod Hedginton the sixteenth at your service."

Perfect. Wolflock smirked. "We need the scenic tour to the inner city, a good place for breakfast, and wherever you recommend for a travel service up the mountain. We need to get to the university before the next season."

"Good golly gosh," Theod flapped his lips and shook his head. "You've come to the right tour guide, then. I know the roads of Mystentine better than anyone. I have made it my life's work to memorise every street, every shop, every mailbox, and its history."

Wolflock smiled at Mothy, whose eyes sparkled.

"We'll get our luggage and meet you at your..." Wolflock gestured to the hansoms outside the stables.

Theod lifted his head as if he were the proudest pony there ever could be. "My buggy is the elegant mahogany one with the blue steel trim. It's the smoothest ride in all of Mystentine and was crafted by the descendants of the oldest blacksmith in the city."

Wolflock looked at Mothy to see if he were excited about the prospect of listening to Theod's tales, and, as the blond boy bounced on the balls of his feet, he knew he could make him forget about his financial troubles with one question.

"And when was your carriage crafted?"

Theod followed them out and began his excited speech about how and when and who crafted the carriage, and their illustrious family histories. Mothy hung off every word as they collected Wolflock's trunks and Mothy's bag, and stacked them on the back of the buggy before they took off into the street.

"Mystentine city is one of the oldest cities in Shiriling but is one of the newer Capital cities in the whole of Puinteyle. Founded by Master Efiar of the Order of the Rewengers, they sought a place of peace and refuge for all those who had been displaced by the Evil King. The two grand walls were built at vastly different times. The first, initially, was defence for the refugees, in the wake of the brutal slaughter of Ravenswood, after they trekked for days and nights over the treacherous Dragon's Spine Mountains. Many of the brave souls froze to death with nowhere to turn until they finally found their way here and claimed this land whence they defeated the Thief King of colours. It is said that the great and noble wizard Margon Corraidhín built these walls with stone shaping magic, but they have since been rebuilt with maintenance. ..."

Mothy prompted Theod with several questions, continuing the running commentary of every monument, every shop, and even of some prominent people walking by. Theod had been honest about knowing as much as he did.

The pair of them looked around at the majestic city

and saw how the magic and science that had been developed in the university for centuries blended so well into the city.

"And what about the university?" Mothy grinned from ear to ear.

"Ah, yes! The university. The main defensive structure of the city. The last bastion of safety during the three wars our city has withheld against. After the Master Thief of Colours was defeated, the people of Mystentine moved into the palace. That's what kept them safe when the worst Winter in recorded history blew through. It was said the snow was so deep that you could walk to Creast on the snow hill that came down from the mountain. It became an official school after that Winter in the years before the fall of the Evil King..."

Wolflock half listened to Theod, but his attention was focused on the sparkles, shines, and saturation of colours flying around the middle city. A dumpy florist with awnings over their stalls brought dried flowers to fragrant life as people asked for them. A man with wings like thin sheets of ice offered tiny potion bottles in steaming teas, saying they would give confidence, energy, and clarity. The temptation to try one of everything, just for the novelty, made him want to stop Theod at every block. But a sensation in his gut nagged at him to get to the travel guide sooner than later.

"Let's go to the inner city, Theod. I heard there's a good bakery and Mothy is starting to fade before my eyes."

"Ah! You mean Leipuri's. Now, I must disclose that she gives me oat rolls for customers I bring to her, but I have always known her bakery to have the best of the best."

Wolflock and Mothy looked at each other with eyebrows raised.

"Far be it from us to deprive you of your well-earned spoils, Sir Theod," Mothy shrugged.

After that, they rode to the inner wall. Wolflock noticed that, although the gates were open, there was more security posted and the magical gemstone locks consisted of the blue stones similarly to the first gate, as well as purple, red and green. The door radiated with wisping stems of magic as the Guards turned the handles. It trailed across their buggy as they passed through it.

"You may not be aware, but the magical glyphs were installed after the walls were built, and the townspeople believed that Evil King sympathisers had infiltrated the town. They're meant to sense ill intent." Theod shook his head, excited to divulge another trivial fact.

"What travel agents are around that could take us up the mountain?" Wolflock asked, noticing that the inner city had far more greenery than the middle city. Fruit trees, herbal shrubs, and berry bushes nestled into every nook and cranny between the townhouses that were woven tightly together.

"Oh, that is a good question, Mr Felen. Good golly gosh, a very good question. As someone who doesn't transcend the mountain, I can name the guides who go up there, but, I must admit, it is getting late in the season, so, if they have shut down for the Winter, I would not be surprised."

"Good to know. Thank you. Let's see them anyway."

"Certainly. The nearest one would be Fjallgöngufólk Tours. They have special paths that they follow to avoid the weather. They'll be a good one."

The little horse took them to an old black building with carved stone statues arching over the door frame. Wolflock and Mothy knocked on the door, but no one answered. Wolflock checked through the window and saw the furniture covered in cloth.

"They've flown for the Winter. I wouldn't be surprised if they are going around the mountains on the Silver Ice Hair." Wolflock pouted.

"On to the next one." Mothy pointed skyward like an intrepid explorer.

Theod moved them on to Sjónamenn Mountaineers, but the address led to a garden with an overgrown stone gazebo. A few people walked through, but the only person sitting in an established fashion was an old lady telling fortunes. She told them her son and his wife normally lead people up the mountain but she had foreseen the weather would be troublesome, so they closed up early in the year.

Wolflock rubbed the place between his eyebrows as his anxiety grew. Suddenly, the welcoming, open arms of Mystentine seemed saccharine, the rich history felt like hyperbole, and the beautiful architecture became a maze.

"Lockie, you look pale. Are you hungry?" Mothy chimed into his thoughts as they made their way back to Theod's buggy.

"No. Let's just keep moving towards the mountain. Theod, where is the next travel guide?"

"There's only one more. Raven's Burrow Mountain Guides, also known as Hrafns Gong Fjaleidsögumenn in Shirth. Some have also claimed that, in an old tongue, it is called Oreb's Hal Ghourn Mrigge. Spooky, no?" the old lady giggled.

Wolflock didn't know what 'old tongue' she was

talking about, but he knew better than to talk in languages he didn't understand. You never knew what you could summon or who was listening.

"Let's go there," Wolflock huffed, his spirits rapidly sinking.

"Leipuri's Pastries is on the way, Mr Enitnelav," Theod reassured them.

"Excellent! I'm starving. Onwards, Theod. Onwards!"

The guards at the first gate were right. The boys smelled the bakery long before they saw it. The delectable aroma of freshly baked bread, cinnamon and honey wrapped itself around them, drawing them closer. If home was a smell, Leipuri's Pastries was it, warm and filled with love. The adorable, shingle sign swung in the shape of a cupcake with "Leipuri's Pastries" painted across it in a sloping cursive.

Most of the other buildings in the inner city were built from stone, but this one resembled the same style as a pretty little cottage, if it had been redesigned into a two-story townhouse. The hand carved edges of the windows framed the display of perfect honey cakes, shaped breads, and cookies with delicate sprinkles, which lined polished wooden shelves sloping towards them in invitation.

Wolflock saw no fingerprints on the glass until Mothy pressed his nose and hands up against them.

"We'll get your oat bread for you, Theod," a blond boy called to the short horse from the bakery door.

Mothy rushed in ahead of Wolflock, tinkling the tiny bell above the door. Wolflock felt the nagging feeling in his stomach begin to bite and he realised it was hunger. Soft bread sprinkled with pine nuts, honey cakes and meringues lined the shelves and glass cabinets like precious jewels. Some even showed dimples of luxury cream and jam fillings.

"In Shellinden, they had a bakery that made cakes into the shape of fish. Have you ever tried salted caramel?" Mothy smacked his lips.

"No, but it does sound good," Wolflock nodded and pulled a few coins from his coin purse as they entered. "I prefer the savoury ones, though. A bit of spice or tang is my favourite."

After a few moments, a happy-faced, chubby lady bounced from the back room to the counter, licking powdered sugar from her perfectly manicured teal nails. "Merry meet, darling hearts. I have just the thing for those aching bellies. Boys like you wake up hungry and stay that way through the whole day." The woman patted down a pristine frilly apron over her teal dress as she drew up a tray of fresh tarts and pies, setting it on the main counter.

Mothy took up one of the custard tarts and bit into it like a goblin. "Thish is delicioush," he sighed in delight.

"Oh, why thank you, honey muffin. I take a lot of pride in our cakes." She swooped her pretty rose-coloured ringlets over her shoulder. Wolflock could barely make out the colour of her eyes; they were so squinted from her smile. "You look like the salty type." She pressed a fingertip to her lips as she analysed Wolflock.

"Tell me about it," Mothy snorted as he tried a jam tart next.

"I have a beautiful, braised lamb in rosemary gravy I think you'd love the chickens out of." She drew out another tray with flaky crust pies.

She can spot what a customer wants in a flash, he thought as he accepted the pie and bit into it.

His stomach sang with delight as the crispy, thin crust and delectable filling soothed his grumpy stomach. Mothy kept talking and chomping until Wolflock made the executive decision to buy him one of everything as well as the biggest sugared chilli scroll, just to teach him spicy could be delicious, too. Mothy looked at him with dewy eyes and threw his arms around his friend in sheer bliss. As he tore into the scroll with abandon, Wolflock felt satiated with his finished pie.

"I take it your partner does the baking?"

"Are you local? I could have sworn you weren't local. My cherub sure does cook them up. He loves his tasty treats nearly as much as I do," She giggled.

"No, ma'am. We're heading up to the university. This is an odd style of building. Very fascinating." Wolflock nodded around the room.

"This used to be the old Bakers Guild. It was set up to prevent nasty competition and help foster good will between all of us. Doesn't stop us from doing good business and offering a little extra sweetness with our service, though." She giggled again with a wink. "We still take students in all the time to learn, though. And we have our seasonal meetings here too. Being good citizens and great bakers. How did you know I wasn't the cook, though?"

Wolflock gave her a crooked, confident smile and leaned on the bench. He realised, if he could get this lady to warm up to him, maybe they would get on track to the University without having any more delays. He wasn't confident in Theod's knowledge to get him up the mountain after two failed agencies.

"I have a particular gift, or so I'm told. I noticed that this fine establishment was filled neatly with all its baked goods and, yet, there is no flour to be seen, except for only a very slight trace leading from the door you came in by. That tells me, given the freshness of the food, the goods are baked out the back in the kitchen, but you don't bake them. You're far too pristine for that. I also noted that your nails are exquisitely done." He smirked, lifting her hand to show her what he saw. "That means that they don't cook, but they count the coins and address the customers, as a good businesswoman does."

The woman giggled and Mothy rubbed his stomach after snarfing his scroll.

"Oh, you little charmer. You already paid for your treats. What can Mrs Leipuri do for you?"

"We're heading up to the University and we've not been through the city before-"

"Say no more. Say no more." She turned and opened draws behind her, looking through cards.

Wolflock's face lit up and he looked eagerly up at Mrs Leipuri. Was she their saviour? Could she give them exactly what they needed to be on their way?

"You muffin cakes need to go and see Ms Vuori. Raven's Burrow Mountain Guides... Let me see. Ahah!" She drew out a pretty card with the picture of a raven with a bright blue eye flying in front of a mountain.

"What?" Wolflock's face fell.

"Oh, aye. Ms Vuori will give you everything you cookies need!"

"Thanks," he sighed.

She didn't respond to his despondency as the bell tinkled above the door while more customers came in, chatting.

"You're most certainly welcome!" she tittered, smiling so much her eyes actually closed.

"And where does Ms Vuori live?" Mothy asked, licking his fingertips of what was left of the scroll.

"Oh she's only a hop, skip and a jump down the lane. Go right down this road, turn left, and she's down the end of Klattrare Lane. You'll see a pretty stained-glass mountain and crow for the sign."

"I'm sure Theod knows the way. Come along, Mothy," Wolflock dragged himself outside in the brisk morning air.

Theod started up his chatting again, but Wolflock tuned it out. Even with the pie in his stomach it churned into knots. Mothy, instead, was still quite distracted by the new town and its fascinating people. They turned down Klattrare street and drew up to the large wooden home, beside a great oak tree. Before the buggy stopped Wolflock jumped out and ran down the path.

A woman wearing a black shawl and black dress

with white hair streaked with black and grey looked like she was locking the door.

"No, no, no!" Wolflock called as his heart raced as fast as his feet. "Please! Please, ma'am? Ms Vuori. We need your help."

The woman's shoulders stiffened, and she bowed her head, making it even harder to see her face.

"Why would I help anyone," she growled with a low, bestial rumble in her throat, "when no one will help me?"

Wolflock opened his mouth to protest, to make an excuse, anything to make her understand his plight. "Ms Vuori, I would like to assist you, but we need to get up to the university before the snow blocks the paths and we'll pay anything you ask to get us there."

Ms Vuori turned her head and glared at him with flaming red eyes, highlighted by her ghostly purple-tinged white skin. Wolflock had never seen a being like her.

"There is no price that can be paid until I get my daughter back."

CHAPTER 2
Overworked, Understaffed

Pardon? We just need to organise-"

"My daughter has gone missing, and I won't be organising any tours until she is back," the woman snapped, flashing sharp teeth. Her pale hands shook as she tried to lock her door. Her thick, dark nails caught on the keyring until she fumbled so badly, she dropped the keys. Wolflock saw that her right hand sported a large masculine gold ring with the same symbol of the crow with a blue eye.

An electric thread flashed through Wolflock's mind.

There was no one better equipped with motive or means to find her child than he was. He needed to get up the mountain. He would find her daughter.

Wolflock crouched down and put his hand over hers on top of the keys. He looked into her crimson eyes, bloodshot from crying, and spoke in his most serious tone, "We will help you find your daughter. Tell me everything."

He stood back up and locked the door with the only key on the ring that was large enough to be a front door key before handing them back to her.

"Are... Are you the officers the Guard sent?" she asked, looking dubious and hopeful. "You're both very young."

"No, ma'am. I'm-"

"This is Wolflock Felen, greatest appraising investigator in all of Puinteyle," Mothy jumped in with a helpful smile. "He's solved cases along the Zilber River, Creast and the road to Mystentine, helping lots of people with problems and mysteries they couldn't solve themselves. Just a few days ago, he helped find a woman who had been lost for forty years and the cure for the disease in the Creast Bay. If there was ever a person to help you find your daughter, it is this man here."

Wolflock's heart swelled with fondness for his dear friend as he spoke, but the woman looked suspicious of his high praise. Seeing her lack of confidence growing, Wolflock glanced over her and the front door of the building.

"I understand your concern for my abilities, Ms Vuori, but I can assure you that I am capable. I often see things others do not, and that goes for the local constabulary as well. For instance, I can see that you are the owner and resident of this establishment by the ring on your hand. Not only does the sign and the door maintain the same symbol, but that ring is an heirloom. The old style is likely to have been created for a man, given its shape, but the worn onyx stones that make up the raven have been scratched. That normally takes extensive, arduous work and a lack of care, or generations of wearing. This building is of a much older style, and you can tell by the rough shape of the chimney that it is far older than the other residences and businesses around it. Knowing Mystentine is a historically significant city, it is safe to assume that it would be passed down to the children of the descendants, rather than being sold off. I would also say that the plaque by your door," he gestured to an old brass plaque by the entrance saying,

By the grace of the mountain gods and the luck of the downtrodden.

We rise above. We rise beyond.
By the strength of will alone we sought our salvation.
May the first to arrive be the last to die.
In memory of those who fell at the slaughter that
brought us here,
Let us remember that with enough courage, wisdom,
and kindness:
All evil can be defeated by love.
                    Efiar, In the 1st Year of Queen Uru'sila

"... that the quoted person would be your ancestor."

She frowned at him and lifted her nose. "Anyone can get that from history books or gossiping around town. I'm reluctant to believe you got all of that from my ring."

"But he did-" Mothy started to defend him, but Wolflock raised his hand to stop him.

"I can also tell that your missing daughter is your only child, as you locked your front door. If someone was within, minding the other children, they would have done this for you. You live a self-sufficient life with no servants or house staff, and you are the one others go to for help. This is why, when you went to the Guard this morning to report your daughter missing and didn't receive the help you wanted, you were more upset than most because you know you would have gone above and beyond for anyone else in your position."

She bit her lip, her shoulders tensing again.

"You also suffer from chronic neck and shoulder tension from carrying these burdens alone. Now, I would not do you the dishonour of aiding you purely through charity. When we find your daughter, all I ask is that my friend and I are guided up the mountain to the university before Winter blocks our way."

Ms Vuori rolled her shoulders, as if testing to see if he was right, then cracked her neck by dropping her pointed pale ears to her shoulders one at a time.

"Fine. Yes. Very well. That's a deal. I'm going back to the Guard station to demand answers. They said they'd contact me by lunch, and that has passed."

"Wonderful." Wolflock rubbed his hands together. "Mothy, let's leave our luggage here. Theod will travel faster if we travel light."

He and Mothy put their things under Ms Vuori's porch seats and jumped into Theod's buggy for the fastest route to the Guard station.

"Now, please tell us everything. Any small detail could be the key to your daughter's whereabouts."

"Ahem." Mothy looked pointedly at Wolflock. "I'm Mothy, Ms Vuori. Would you like us to address you like that? And, also, what is your daughter's name?"

Ms Vuori swallowed back her anxiety and tears as she gathered her thoughts. "Lija. My little girl is Lija. She's only a decade old. She's turning eleven in two months. When I woke up this morning, I called her down for breakfast. She's getting to the age where she sleeps in a lot, some days as late as lunch, so I thought she was still snoozing. I brought her breakfast to her, but she wasn't there and her window was open. I rushed to the Guard station first thing this morning, but I could only find one man there. I gave him my statement and he said officers would be along around lunchtime to investigate. They never arrived. While I waited, I sent letters to my sister and Lija's father. I asked everyone up and down the street and several lanes over if they had seen or heard anything, but no one had any information. They're all worried and looking for me in the lanes over."

"It sounds like a friendly community." Mothy patted her arm.

"It is. Everyone knows everyone. Each suburb is like its own big family, and we all help each other. That's how I was able to raise Lija these last five years by myself. It's Lija who is the sociable one. She always comes home with dishes from the neighbours when I'm working late, and sends them back filled with something just as tasty. She's very independent." Ms Vuori broke down and wept into her hands. Mothy put his arm around her slender shoulders and comforted her until she could speak again.

"When was the last time you saw her?" Wolflock asked, trying to be as delicate as Mothy. "And did your sister or Lija's father get back to you?"

"Yesterday evening at dinner. She likes to work on her projects in her room after dinner and it's nice to see her focused, so I let her have her privacy while I read in the family room." She dug through her dress pockets until she found a tightly crumpled ball of paper. "Her father sent me this. My sister hasn't sent me word yet."

It was hardly a letter and more a stress ball made of paper. Wolflock uncrumpled the parchment and smoothed it out.

To Kiipei Vuori

You haven't spoken to me in months and the first thing you ask is "have you stolen our daughter"? Ludicrous! No I have not. This had better be a sick joke. Lija means the world to me. Please agree to see me so we can look for her together.

Yours always, Uskoton Dalur

The phrasing in the letter seemed peculiar. On one hand, he was very formal with certain words, and then insulting and volatile with others. Was it just fatherly stress? Given their separation and Ms Vuori only referring to him as "Lija's father", Wolflock guessed that they had a strained relationship. She had earlier said she raised Lija by herself for five years out of the eleven the child had seen, meaning that the father had likely done something to cause the separation back then. The last line in the note had a sense of desperation to reconnect. Searching separately would have been far more logical as they could cover more ground.

"What was the cause of your separation five years ago?" he asked, folding the note.

Ms Vuori scowled. "His wife came to live here from Quarenth."

"Were you aware of his... relations?"

"Of course not! Filthy pig spent years wooing me, even raising a daughter and building a business together, only to turn around on my birthday and tell me his wife was arriving shortly. Apparently, she wanted to live in Mystentine to be close to him. I should have known he was lying to me this whole time. With his months of 'business trips' and his constant secrets!" her face contorted with rage as she spoke with absolute venom. "If I didn't love my business and my daughter, I would have left a long time ago. I don't know how the other woman stays with him.

Once a liar, always a liar. I would have been fine with it all had he told us both the truth from the start. At least we could have come to an understanding. But she hates Lija and I. She's one of those Troston raised women and only believes in strict monogamy; 'until death do they part'. If she could, she'd be rid of both of us for good."

Both young boys looked at each other uncomfortably through her outburst, but they couldn't disagree with her.

"It's just a basic lesson, isn't it?" Mothy strained a smile to placate her. "All children are taught that lies do horrible things. Like leaving warts on your tongue."

"They tie you in an inescapable web, so, to maintain one such as this without seeking understanding from all parties involved is disastrous." Wolflock shrugged with his clinical logic. "What does your daughter look like?"

Ms Vuori took a breath. "She's the mirror image of me, but with less lines on her face, and she is only this tall." She held her hand out at chest height. "She often carries her black backpack around for errands. She's a good runner and her backpack was specially made by my mother for her. It's light and durable and bears our family crest."

She held out her hand to show them the large gold ring with a shiny obsidian shaped into a raven with its bright blue eye.

"Black birds are fairly common," Wolflock shrugged

as he continued to look at the ring.

"Not this one. Ravens are sacred to most in Mystentine. They followed our ancestors from Ravenswood over the mountains and helped them find food, water, and shelter until they settled here. Our ravens have bright blue eyes. Most ravens have black eyes. It was through the breeding of owls and our ravens that we helped create the postal system of crowls."

"Silent fliers but intelligent?" Wolflock asked, wondering what that combination could possibly look like.

"Exactly. They're fast too."

"So we're looking for a young girl who looks like you with a backpack that has this symbol on it?" Mothy asked, looking over her ring.

Ms Vuori nodded. "It's embroidered with black and blue wire, so it shines."

"And what did her day consist of yesterday?" Wolflock asked.

Again, Ms Vuori took a breath, this time closing her eyes as she thought. "We woke up like usual. I rise at dawn and prepare breakfast, then we eat together. Lija was more tired than normal. She'd been up all night writing in her little adventure diary. I got to work on the reports for the last two trips up to the mountain and the others through the city, making sure our guides were organised. Lija went on her errands. She had to take my sister her medication, and she had a lot of letters to take to the post office. Her and her friends like to write little riddles to each other." As she spoke Wolflock noticed a hesitation in her voice. "Then, she came home, and we ate dinner."

"And what else?" He raised a dark eyebrow at her.

Ms Vuori clenched her fists on the buggy seat so hard her knuckles went white. "I asked her to not go to her father's home. She's a good girl, but she always does whatever she wants, and she loves her father dearly. I wouldn't be surprised if she found her way there yesterday and didn't tell me. That's why I asked her father if he saw her yesterday, but you can see by his note that he hasn't answered the question."

"I will keep a note of that. Theod, how much longer until we reach our destination?"

The short horse bobbed his head as he thought for a moment. "Four more lanes over, Mr Felen. We'll be there as the crowl flies. Speaking of silent flight, did you know one of my ancestors was known to have incredibly quiet hooves and helped lead the refugees from Grothener through to Mystentine in the years leading up to Queen Uru'sila's rule? They were said to display tremendous resilience and survived the mountainous journey with only three blades of grass, some pine leaves, and by licking snow."

Wolflock tuned out Theod again and began counting the lamp posts, tailors, and scribes as they clickety-clacked towards the Guard station. The station sat in a large plot consisting of four towers surrounding a squat central spire in a green field where people trained their bodies.

"The Mystentine Guard Headquarters and Training grounds used to be the barracks after the mountain became too hard to train troops on. This was the original keep built to protect the few people who had first settled here over one thousand years ago. Large enough to house just over one thousand people snugly with all the food, weapons, armour, livestock and resources needed to bunker down, this was a particular feat of the ingenuity of the desperate." Theod continued with his running commentary as he drove them down the smooth road leading to the main offices.

The training grounds were filled with people practising their various exercises to keep their bodies in peak condition. Drills, laps, and obstacle courses were all in use as grey clad folk of all shapes and sizes performed athletic feats. As they drew closer to the main tower, he saw newer buildings had been added to the main one, giving room for classes. Through the windows into the newer buildings he could see classes, record halls, and rooms where people were tending to their equipment. All of them wore variations of a deep blue uniform with a cream undershirt, emblazoned with a shining, embroidered gold dragon head.

"Huh... The uniform is different in other countries. In Grothener the dragon head is silver." Wolflock noted to Mothy.

"It's gold in Shellinden too. There're a lot of werewolves in the Guard down there and they don't want them to get hurt on duty," his friend responded.

Theod snorted happily. "The dragon was a mystical symbol of a creature with immense intelligence, understanding, compassion and power. It had been the Great Queen Uru'sila's most beloved creature, and one she had entrusted to those who were willing to support the community and serve those who needed them most. From experience, most of the Guard are given mediation training first, then are sent back to their communities to help balance conflicts, always enabling both disputing parties to feel like they had come out even. Balance, fairness and diplomacy is the motto of all the Guards. To serve the community and all the people in it. Good golly gosh, it's such a noble occupation."

Wolflock sighed. As noble as that sounded, he was all too familiar with those that were weak willed and self-absorbed amongst the Guard and those they protected in

Plugh.

Theod drew them through the courtyard and around to the entrance to the central tower. As they got out of the buggy, Wolflock saw classes being held where civilians were being taught by the Guards. He glimpsed a trust-fall exercise and remembered dropping one of the Thorn brothers on purpose to teach them a lesson when he'd been made to do it in Plugh. Wolflock also noticed that there appeared to be a high density of civilians in regular clothes demanding attention. Groups around him anxiously reported thefts and assault, while others were hauled through in shackles, stumbling as they struggled.

"There is the office you're after. I'll wait here for when you're done," Theod said, raising a hoof towards one of the squarish buildings built onto the main tower.

The three of them stepped out of the carriage and their shoes crunched on the loose gravel leading up to the little side building. The grey, faded sign above the door read "Division of Child Protection and Investigation".

Wolflock knocked and opened the door, curious about why it wasn't open like many of the other department doors were. He heard someone swear from within as something crashed to the floor. An older man had risen from his chair and, as he did, his clerk had tripped behind him, sending files and papers scattering around the small office.

That wasn't the only thing out of place in the dishevelled office. Waste bins around the room were filled with crumpled balls of paper, investigation string laid strewn across the floor as if highly active kittens had tried their paws at solving clues, and chairless desks sat stacked with brown manilla folders. Only three desks had names on them; Captain H.J. Estivan, Officer B. Tand, and the last one had a handwritten paper insert saying "Administration Chestir Moi'ez" next to a piled up ashtray.

"Tand, help Chestir clean this up." The older man gripped his curly auburn hair as the young lady with short spiky brown hair raced forward, slapping the clerk's hands off the pile while she scooped up the papers. The older man turned to Wolflock, Mothy and Ms Vuori. "I'm so sorry, we're a bit snowed under. How can I assist?"

Ms Vuori stammered as her face grew dark purple, "How can you assist? I've been waiting since dawn for your team to send someone down! My daughter has been missing since last night and you act as if you haven't even started looking for her!"

The man Wolflock assumed to be Captain Estivan paled. "My deepest apologies. Ma'am, let me see if Chestir or Tand can find your file." Tand's amber eyes shot up, ready to jump to action as her captain spoke. "In the meantime, can you relay what has happened?"

"I gave it all to a thin man with short dark hair this morning, and I just told these boys the same-"

"A dark-haired thin man? I'm sorry ma'am. You must have been in a different building. It's just the three of us here."

Ms Vuori clenched her fist again. "No, I wasn't. I was right here in this office. This is the only place to report a missing child. I was here at dawn."

Captain Estivan looked up at the ginger haired man with thick glasses that magnified his eyes like an insect. "Chestir, you were here first this morning. Did you take this woman's statement or see the person that did?"

"N-No sir. I came a little later than usual b-because I thought I was ahead in my work. I didn't see anyone," Chestir stammered as he picked up the files, bumping his hand with Officer Tand as he tried to help. She snapped at him with a bark and and glared him down until he returned the papers to the floor for her to sort.

Captain Estivan sighed, drawing out new paperwork for Ms Vuori. "You wouldn't happen to be Lija's mother, would you?"

Wolflock, Mothy and Ms Vuori froze. "Y-yes. I am. Do you know her?" Her face had just started to fade back to white when it started to flare up again. "Do you know my daughter?"

Captain Estivan looked at Officer Tand with an expression Wolflock could only describe as regret. "Lija has been asking myself and Officer Tand for mentoring. She hoped to get into the Guard when she was older, and, in her training, she has been running errands. Mostly helping us get food, medicine, and shelter to the street children. This... this is devastating for all of us to learn."

Ms Vuori stifled a sob. "I... I had no idea. She just said she went out on adventures. Oh, my girl. My beautiful girl. Was she in any danger working for you?"

Captain Estivan shook his head. "None whatsoever. Her work involved going from one secure station to another. I... I'm sorry to admit it, but I thought she was just another street child or a foster child. She seemed very clever. Again, I am terribly sorry for this mix up. I will dedicate Officer Tand to your case immediately and it will be her number one priority. Missing children always take priority."

"B-b-but sir." Chestir shook. "We have the mayor's special case about the increase in adolescent smoking and the West wall graffiti racket, as well as the seven break ins from last night-"

Captain Estivan raised his hand and Chestir fell silent. "Missing children always take priority, Chestir. All of that can wait. Even the mayor. And this is Lija. She's important to all of us."

"Yes, sir. Sorry, sir. I forgot myself."

"Well, you'd best go find yourself and your manners. Make sure these files are in the right folders and request assistance from the cadets. Now, Ms Vuori, was it?" Captain Estivan pushed the folders on his left further to the side, sending a few sliding off the desk. Mothy's rapid reflexes caught them before they fell into the heaped waste bin. "What can you tell me about your daughter's disappearance?"

As Ms Vuori went through her tale again, Wolflock looked around the room. The wooden walls were covered from ceiling to dado rail with missing item posters, wanted graffiti artists, bullies, and missing persons from other departments. A bowl with only a few shiny pink candies sat on the guest side of the desk. He saw each desk had a similar bowl, but only three had any presence of the hard candy.

Out of the five desks, three were in constant use, one looked as if it were used purely for storage, but the last one had a place cleared where someone had been working on something recently. Besides the door they came through, there were two doors leading into other rooms.

Officer Tand opened the first door into a little

kitchen and lunchroom that had also become storage, with mountains of folders and papers stacked against the walls. The folders were bundled with a distinct red string Wolflock noticed was only on Officer Tand's desk.

Ah... He thought to himself, *She's in charge and makes sure no one touches the filing system. I'm glad Myna isn't here. She'd find ways to sneak these things around anyway.*

She made Ms Vuori a cup of relaxing tea by turning a red gemstone in a slot on the kettle. It made it whistle, but, as she caught Wolflock's eye while he watched her, the gemstone shot out at rapid speed and shattered against the wall.

"Captain? Can you order a new hot stone?"

Captain Estivan groaned, putting his tired face in his hands. "You can get one when you go to Ms Vuori's home to investigate, Officer."

"Yes, sir."

"And these boys have to join us," Ms Vuori said quickly, not taking a sip of her tea. "I need everyone I can working on this."

"Uh... Listen, ma'am, I know you're worried about your child, but-"

"No. Tand. She's right. A few extra eyes will help. They'll go with you as Ms Vuori's company. Find every location Lija went to over the last two days. There are very few travellers in town besides students heading up before Winter. We're understaffed enough as it is. Dig around the warehouses and the apothecary, and make sure you contact her father."

"Sir." Chestir stood up with a stiff back and looked as if he were about to salute. "I would also like to be of assistance. I could go with Officer Tand and take all the notes necessary so that she can think on her feet. I can also report back if these... guests... are interfering with the investigation."

Captain Estivan considered the proposal, but Tand jumped in first. "That won't be necessary, sir. I'm perfectly fine to take all my own notes. I don't need the help. I'll have enough on my hands with Ms Vuori and her friends."

"Very well, officer. Report back this evening by note or person. Dismissed."

With admirable determination, Officer Tand collected her work belt and a file, and held the door for Ms Vuori, Mothy and Wolflock to leave.

"You're not fond of Chestir's affections?" Wolflock smirked as they made their way back to Theod's buggy.

"Ah. I see you do have powers of observation. That will be useful. Ms Vuori, we need to see Lija's room first, so please take us back to your home. We'll begin there." Tand shook her head back as if she had long hair, looking like a filly with a trimmed mane.

She's cut her hair recently and gone much shorter than she is used to, He looked her over for indications that she was upset with them being there, but if she was, it was overshadowed by her happiness being out of the office.

"What's in that file? You didn't have one on Lija before we came in. What is of importance in there?" Wolflock asked bluntly as Theod took off again.

"That's for me to know and for you to prove you can put more clues together than a one-sided office romance."

Rhiannon D. Elton

CHAPTER 3

The Room of a Natural Snoop

The buggy ride back to the Raven's Burrow Mountain Tours was cramped between the four of them. A few times Mothy had to hang on to Wolflock in order to keep the dark haired boy from falling off the side. Wolflock showed no signs of displeasure at the journey. On the contrary, he had to keep swallowing back the smile that tried to creep onto his face. Not only was he going to get what they needed to ascend the mountain, but he was also going to solve a new puzzle.

Wolflock hid his excitement mostly because whenever Mothy caught a glimpse of him, his eyes flashed a warning brown. He could tell his friend didn't like him seeming pleased while a child was missing.

Theod stopped outside the gate, and Wolflock noticed that most of the properties closest to the mountain had green yards. The Vuori's had two ancient, knobbly trees on either side of their front path, with posters outlining the rules of hiking up the mountain.

"What is the schedule for the mountaineers? When did the last ones leave and how frequently do they depart?" Wolflock asked as they stepped onto the porch. Mothy checked over their luggage, but none of it appeared to be tampered with.

"Can I just pop these inside, Ms Vuori?"

"Huh? Yes. Now, listen. You said you'd help first before I organised your venture up the mountain." She frowned as she unlocked the front door.

"That's not what I meant. When did the last expeditions leave and when are they expected to return? Could Lija have left with them?"

"No. That's not possible. We have one team that goes up the mountain to the university and the other goes around in a loop to show the best views in Shiriling. The one to the university takes a week round trip and the loop takes three weeks. The university trip is waiting to leave in the next few days, and the round trip is due back this afternoon before sunset."

Wolflock nodded, taking that mental thread from his web. The four of them entered the old house and Wolflock thought it looked like a museum. The entrance hall held the flight of stairs leading up to the second story. The ancient, worn carpet looked like it used to be red but had faded to a pale brown. The mid-sized paintings lining the walls captured moments between the generations that lived here, as did the furniture. Centuries old side tables mixed with modern coat racks told him a possible motive for kidnapping Lija could have been generational wealth, given the only people currently in town were well known unless they were travelling to the university. It also told him that the Vuori's were practical people who weren't phased by fashion.

Ms Vuori led them to the parlour to the right of the entrance hall, and Wolflock admired the seats of intricately embroidered velvet. In the middle of the room stood a stone table with an unused hookah. The whole room seemed out of place compared to the exterior and entranceway.

"You help a lot of traders from Uluken go up to the University, don't you, Ms Vuori?" Wolflock asked as she scribbled a note for the guide returning this evening.

"Aye. They all want to get up there to sell to the University. Most reliable deals they can get. I keep everything in this room to make them comfortable while we discuss prices and procedures. But why do you ask?"

"Can you tell me anything else about your daughter? Did she help you with these guests?" Wolflock ignored her question. Had the girl run off with a merchant or taken something to them that they'd left behind?

Ms Vuori's pointed nose twitched as if she were about to cry again. "She's still alive but I know she's in some kind of trouble." She looked as human as an elf, and less so with her features creased from being distraught. Everything about her looked sharper and more predatory than regular humans.

"Forgive me, ma'am, but how do you know that? Perhaps she is tending to your merchant customers somewhere?"

"We haven't had any through since early Autumn. I can tell because I have a connection to those in my bloodline. I can tell she is unharmed, but her fear is my fear, and I can feel her trying to be brave. I feel sick." Ms Vuori wept into her hands.

Wolflock looked at Mothy and Officer Tand, who

shrugged, looking uncomfortable.

"You'll have to forgive me, again. Is there something magically gifted about your race?"

Ms Vuori stopped crying and wiped her face with a sigh. "You're not from Mystentine. I forget that other countries don't have Antrum. Most people around here know the history of the Antrum. We're called under elves as slang for those that remember it. I suppose there really aren't many of us left. I only know of a handful in Shiriling and the ones remaining all came here after the Last King destroyed us."

The boys stayed silent and let her continue.

"The Antrum were a powerful race that was nearly wiped out by the Evil King. I'm not going to go into my history, but, I will say that we see better in the dark, we're always magically inclined, and we can somewhat sense and control our descendants through a form of ancient blood magic. Only the strongest and most ruthless can control others against their will through blood magic. I only use mine to make sure Lija is safe. Some days, it's more of a torment than a gift." She began weeping again. Mothy knelt next to her, patting her back.

"I'll need to see her room. Where is it?"

Ms Vuori pressed her lips tightly together and nodded, gathering herself before she took them through the hall and upstairs. The large house had many bedrooms and craft rooms. Lija's room overlooked one of the streams coming down from the mountain at the back of the house. The room itself was unlike any children's room Wolflock had seen.

Except his own.

Hand drawn pictures pinned to the walls were joined by decorated strings. Some strings had little paper stars, while others had kitten faces. Dates, times, names, and other details accompanied the brightly coloured drawings. Lija recorded things meticulously.

Many of the pictures showed her and her friends in front of red brick buildings with strings of graffiti at shoulder height. Some of the circled children had purple faces and then had no other pictures of them after that date. Another few pictures were the children burying purple bags outside the city walls. Wolflock had a sneaking suspicion he knew where this was going. Ten missing children, and, finally, a picture showing one child blowing a purple cloud into another child's face as they did a strange chicken impression.

Lija found people using Lady Mind Master to abduct children. They found a store of it and buried it. Smart girl.

"I tell her to clean her room up, but she just loves

this stringy mess," Ms Vuori inhaled sharply.

"It's a perfect chaos, isn't it?" Wolflock mumbled to himself.

Lija's clothes and shoes were strewn around the floor in piles, but Wolflock could see the piles were for different occasions. One pile for outdoor activities, one for formal occasions, one for business, and another with black clothes and no shoes, only thick black socks. Was Lija participating in nefarious nighttime activities?

Half-finished cups of water sat wherever Lija had worked for any duration. Even with the mess, it was evident that there hadn't been an altercation in the room. He found a pink lolly stuck to a sleeve, and then a small bag of them behind a cup at her desk. Her desk was a small, whitewashed writing desk with three lockable drawers.

Wolflock scoffed. The draws themselves were locked but the keys were left in the keyholes. A rookie mistake that Wolflock remembered teaching Myna about when he'd read her letters to a boy who had tried to express an interest in her. She obliviously broke his heart and didn't realise until Wolflock read her responses back to her. At dinner. In front of their father.

Various papers covered her desk, along with more rough drawings, letters back and forth from friends at school and receipts for her aunt's medicine from a Växtadlare Apothecary.

"Boring, boring, boring," Wolflock muttered, then turned his attention to the drawers. Letters addressed to Lija from her father.

As Wolflock flipped through them, he noted the dates. They corresponded daily up until yesterday. They weren't in order and some of the sweeter ones had been brought to the front, most likely to be read over and over. At the bottom of each page was a strange scrawling picture that changed from letter to letter. Sometimes it was repeated, but it looked like someone had tried to write a sentence and draw an image at the same time.

Wolflock squinted. He'd seen this somewhere before. Where had it been? It was so familiar.

"Did she have many friends?" Mothy asked as Wolflock stared at the letters from Lija's father. Officer Tand stepped over the clothes and looked at the papers with Wolflock.

"Oh yes. Everyone loves Lija. She's bright and friendly and welcoming to anyone she meets. Even the kids who cause trouble, you know? I think they were all fascinated by her being an Antrum. Some people choose our services just to ask us questions about our heritage. She takes it all with a good nature, though."

"Could she be staying at a friend's house?" Mothy asked.

"I went and saw them all this morning and spread the word through town but none of her school friends had seen her. I came home looking for any sign of where she could have gone. I couldn't bear to touch her room though," Ms Vuori choked. "What if I never see my baby again? What if this is the only memory I have of her now?" Ms Vuori wept again and Mothy hugged her. "If only that useless Corlman would take this seriously!"

Corl...

"Her father is from Corl?" Wolflock's eyes shot to Ms Vuori.

She nodded in confusion.

He quickly grabbed the pencil from the desk and began scribbling above the odd drawings on the father's letters.

"Hah! It's Corlesian! Pictographic code, but it's definitely Corlesian! M... E... E..." he breathed as he began to see what they said. It was as if someone had removed a veil from his mind. "Meet me at my work at mid-morning for pie... Meet me at my work at sunrise for breakfast... I have a surprise for you. Meet me at my work at dusk... They're all in code! She was meeting her father in secret every day for the last month at his work or nearby. Where does he work?"

Wolflock's heart skipped at his puzzle solving genius.

"In the non-perishables warehouses by the back of the district. Do you think she may be there?"

"Well, it's the only consistent meeting place. It's a clue and we need to examine it thoroughly." His pen scratched rapidly as he deciphered the messages. "I can see here that she would meet him whenever he had a night shift. We need to see these warehouses. That's where she's been sneaking off to most nights. That's where the majority of these pictures depict. If she wasn't there to see her father, she was there helping the children that lurked around there. Now, what I want to know is why were so many troubled children lurking around the warehouses, and why do you look so shocked that she was seeing her father, Ms Vuori?"

CHAPTER 4
Secrets in Storage

"I-I told her she could only see her father here."

"And why was that?" Wolflock folded the letters and eyed Ms Vuori.

"Last Summer, Lija came home from her father's house with bruises down her arms and she refused to tell me how she got them. I can tell a handprint when I see one though. If she'd told me it was his wife, I would have made an arrangement, but her secrecy made me suspect it could have been her father. I told them he could see her here, but his wife refuses to let him come here."

"So, you're at an impasse."

"For Lija's safety!" Ms Vuori protested.

"I'll get Theod ready," Mothy said loudly.

"I don't doubt that, Ms Vuori. In order to find Lija, you have to be completely transparent with all information. A detail like that gives me far more insight into the situation if we were to see Mr or Mrs Dalur. Everything can be a clue, and every clue can be the difference between finding Lija or not."

"I understand," she said, unable to lift her eyes to meet his.

As the three of them descended the stairs, Tand caught Wolflock's arm. "You are as subtle as a brick. Clever, but ruthless."

Wolflock couldn't tell if she meant that to be a compliment or an insult, but her half-cocked smirk made him feel like she was looking for something in him. Instead of letting the file she brought hang loosely by her side, Officer Tand had tucked it up under her arm. She trusted him less.

"Let me get this straight for you," he turned to face her dead on. "My goal for months has been to get to the top of that mountain and enrol in the university." He pointed to the mountainside wall. "She is the last travel guide who can take me up there and she refuses to do so until her daughter is found. No. I don't care about her feelings. Why should I? Especially if they're going to get in the way. I don't know why you're more guarded than before, but I can assure you that my methods work and you withholding information is only going to make this harder. It may even prevent us from successfully finding her."

"Lija means a lot to all of us. She's a special kid. I just want to make sure you aren't on the other team."

"Other team?" Wolflock frowned as Officer Tand walked by him and out of the door. "What do you mean, other team?"

She got onto the buggy without another word and started up a conversation with Mothy to stop Wolflock from asking any questions as they drove into the storage and manufacturing suburbs.

The buildings became more plain, all built of the same, dusty red brick with large wooden barn doors. Many of them were loosely latched with a bolt and chain, while others had grey paved stairs leading up to small, windowed offices. Theod regaled them with stories of important living standards and workers conditions being discussed in these very streets, but Wolflock tuned him out faster than before.

There were no signs that people lived in the area.

No washing lines, no smells of cooking, no decorations on the outside of the buildings. The monotonous buildings only varied by what could be seen through the windows and the engraved names above doorways. Eventually Ms Vuori pointed out the building marked "*595 Fjallafoss Warehouses and Storage*".

"Saraesh is the other manager. Her and Lija's father went into business for this place a couple of years before his wife came to town."

"And they still do shift work here? As if they were staff?" Wolflock asked.

"Uskoton says it helps them understand their employees' conditions better and takes the pressure off when they're understaffed for whatever reason. After his wife came up here, I thought he was lying in order to have affairs, but Saraesh wouldn't lie to me. We'd been friends for years before she went into business."

I'll be the judge of that, Wolflock thought to himself as they walked through the front doors.

He'd never been too familiar with the working class. After his mother went missing, his father kept him and Myna on the property for most of their time. He also held most of his business meetings in the house, restricting Wolflock's knowledge of the general populace to what walked in the door. As he entered the warehouse reception area, he had an overwhelming wave of realisation wash over him.

Ah. It all makes sense.

The durable clothing, sturdy boots, traces of mud and silt. It all belonged here. This was the natural habitat of all those clues and their origins.

The woman leaning over the workbench desk didn't look up at them as they came in. She just kept writing in the ledger with a tanned hand that stood out in the climate that raised pale skinned folk.

"You have until I finish this line to tell me why you're here and what you want. I'm about to start my rounds." She tapped her pen to get more ink out. "Oh, Kiipei? What brings you to this neck of the woods?"

"Saraesh, has Lija been around today? I know she's been seeing her father here some nights," Ms Vuori gripped the other side of the workbench desk to hold herself steady.

"I take it you weren't aware. I thought it was weird Uskoton wanted all the night shifts he could get. We reorganised my nights for weekends and Sollempus and he took the other four. That man hasn't got the mind for day paperwork." She blew across the ink, tinkling the delicate gold chain of trinkets running from her nostril to her earlobe.

Ms Vuori let out a nervous laugh.

"When was the last time you saw Lija?" Officer Tand stepped forward, crossing her arm in Wolflock's way as he tried to do the same.

Saraesh's lips pinched, and her eyes slid away from the group in front of her, "Umm... maybe a few weeks now. Why? What's happened?"

Wolflock tilted his head. She was lying. He could tell by her tone and change in posture. She was uncomfortable with the lie.

"Lija's gone missing. She wasn't in her bed when I woke up this morning." Ms Vuori's voice cracked.

Officer Tand patted Ms Vuori's back before turning to Saraesh. "Do you know anything about where she could be?"

"Have you spoken with Uskoton yet?" she asked Ms Vuori, glancing back and forth anxiously and tried to ignore Tand's question.

She doesn't want to incriminate her business partner, Wolflock narrowed his eyes.

"He sent a message saying he didn't know where she was. He was scheduled for last night, yes?" Officer Tand asked.

Wolflock watched Saraesh's expression closely. Her brows pinched in confusion. "Umm... he was, but he asked me at the last moment to cover his shift. He had important family matters going on, he said."

"Can you show us where Mr Uskoton goes about his work?" said officer Tand.

"No," Wolflock waved his hand in irritation. "No, we won't need that. What I'd like to know is where you saw Lija and her father last night."

All eyes stared wide at Wolflock.

"Care to elaborate, genius?" Officer Tand scoffed.

"Yes. If you couldn't tell Saraesh lied about the last time she saw Lija, you're a fool. Her posture changed, her voice dropped, and she didn't give details. Classic signs of lying, especially when the change is so dramatic. The same shift happened when she mentioned Uskoton asking for the night off last night, and, yet, she's confused because she is sure she saw him and Lija outside. Now, were you tired last night because you had to pull a double shift, or are you lying to protect someone?"

Mothy sighed, "You may as well tell him. He gets that look, knows he's right and, if you resist, he'll dredge up worse things."

"Now, now, Mothy. You'll spoil my fun if you give away the game." Wolflock chuckled.

Ms Vuori looked furiously between them as they spoke, and Officer Tand flared red with indignation.

"Was it him? It was him, yes?" Saraesh paled.

"Show us the place and we'll see if it was." Wolflock gestured to the door leading out the back.

Saraesh opened it and showed them out. Their business rented out twelve identical sheds lined up in a four across and three along formation. Workers used trolleys and hand carts to transport trunks, barrels, crates, and other containers to and from the sheds.

"What do you normally store in these?" Wolflock asked.

"Building materials, exports from Mystentine like pine furniture, some people hire it out for storage, but they have to need it for a lot. We won't hire out if it's for strange items or things that aren't worth the rental. Just in case they never pay up."

The lanes between the warehouses were mostly clear, but a few had crates and boxes sitting along the walls marked with a large red stamp, marking the contents as broken or spoiled. Graffiti below shoulder height covered the sheds. Wolflock could see an overlap in the paint. The older drawings had obvious depictions of childish, crude images that could have been quite offensive, painted over again with far more savoury and artistic images, although only slightly better in skill.

Lija convinced the street children to paint images

her father would have approved of. Artistic expression and helping the local youths. Smart or compassionate?

"Think about how much fun a young imagination could have in these parts." Mothy drummed his hands over every flat surface he could as they walked through the lane. "Pretending to be a sailor or an adventurer, climbing over boxes that could be mountains, hiding in barrels that were caves, finding lost treasure in the form of broken bits and trinkets."

"But there are no children here, Mothy." Wolflock scanned the area.

"None of them have been around for a few weeks," Saraesh said as she took out her keys for the warehouses, showing them the inside of the sheds through little sliding viewers. "We don't stock non-perishables here. That warehouse is in the middle city. Kids normally like sweets and things to eat rather than building supplies. Here's where I saw her and her pa."

Saraesh stopped down the third lane and gestured to a cluster of boxes by the second row, shed number six.

"Was this their regular meeting place?" Officer Tand asked.

Wolflock looked up and saw the crates were the furthest they could be from the corner lights on the sheds. They may have been in complete darkness.

"No. She would normally come into the office. Uskoton has notebooks for her to write her little notes in, as well as a stack of candies."

"It must have been a very serious discussion," Wolflock mumbled to himself, looking at the crates. Little scuff marks from where she kicked her heels told him where she sat, but the larger one next to it had blue wool fibres caught on it. Much like the coat Officer Tand wore.

The odd evidence made Wolflock wary of the plucky Guardswoman.

"What time did you see them here?" the officer asked.

"It was before midnight. That's why I thought it was strange to see them there. Normally, when she's here this early, she stays all evening, and he drops her back home before sunrise. I had to ask him to not take her himself because he would leave the warehouses unguarded while he went, and we had a break in. That's why I thought he would have taken her home last night. Maybe they just needed to talk in private."

"What was stolen when you had your break in?" Officer Tand took out her notepad and began writing things down.

"That was the strange thing. They stole my set of

keys and we had to have all the locks changed. They never managed to steal anything. It set our reputation back a bit, though. I thought it might have been our old admin boy. He vanished for a week, but then came back saying he'd had a family emergency. Then he left a month later."

"When did you have the locks reset? And did you have the Mystentine Guard here while the locks were being changed?" Wolflock asked before Tand could push in.

"It was a year ago. And no. They weren't." Saraesh eyed him carefully.

Wolflock put the blue wool in his journal with a note about its location. The sky over them had turned to a dusty pink, highlighting what looked like glass beads wedged between the crates.

Wolflock jammed his hand between them and pinched them out, passing them to Mothy. "Lollies?"

"Mmm... Pink candies covered in sugar. Curious. There's something else back here too." Wolflock laid belly down on the crate and tugged at a sturdy fabric wedged between the wooden boxes. Mothy grabbed his legs to give him better leverage.

With a final yank he freed it. A backpack. The double strapped bag had a flap with a wire embroidered black raven and blue eye.

Had Lija hidden this here while she spoke with her father?

Ms Vuori gasped, bursting into fresh tears. Saraesh hugged her, keeping the mother's back to the scene.

Officer Tand tried to snatch the bag away, but Wolflock gave her a stern look and let his piercing blue eyes do what they did best. Officer Tand folded her arms and gestured for him to open it in front of her.

Wolflock ran his hand through the bag and found two receipts for two bags of medicine from the Växtadlare Apothecary. His fingers stuck to a small white paper bag of pink lollies, these ones smooth and uncoated. They had melted together into a lump. From the sticky lollies clinging to his fingers, a folded piece of paper stuck to them. He shook his hand a few times, but it wouldn't unstick.

Officer Tand peeled it off with a smirk and shook it out. "It's dated for yesterday."

"It has that funny writing down the bottom," Mothy poked the note, his sticky finger clinging to it. "Do you think it's from her father?"

"It wasn't him," Wolflock frowned and held the note close to his face.

Mixed with the scent of iron-based ink and

parchment was something floral. Some kind of essential oil or perfume. The ink was even thinner where a creamed hand had run along it on the right-hand side. The writing itself was shaky and showed a lot of hesitation. Unlike the boldness of Lija's father's other letters with their broad, heavy-handed strokes, this letter looked as if Uskoton was writing with a broken finger or a severe burn on his hand, making him wince away from the page after every few words. The little flicks trailing off the end of the words told him that. The spacing was also irregular, as if every time the writer got into the flow of the sentence they would stop and reset.

My darling Lija,

These words were the only ones pressed firmly into the page. The indent could be felt on the other side. Was Uskoton angry about addressing his child?

I miss you terribly and I have fantastic news that I need to tell you. I can't address it here, in case someone finds this letter, but you must keep it very secret. I know it will surprise you when you finally know it. I love you dearly and cannot wait to meet when your mother is in a better frame of mind.

Your doting father, Uskoton.

Beneath the writing was the secret code. This scribble was written with far more confidence, but with an elegance that Uskoton's firm hand hadn't shown before.

Meet me by the warehouse in the usual spot after supper. I don't know when I'll be there so you may have to wait a while. Don't worry though; I'll come, even late in the morning.

"She took this note with her..." Wolflock breathed, pinching his chin between his thumb and forefinger.

Ms Vuori approached and Mothy moved back so she could read it over Officer Tand's shoulder. Mothy looked around as if it would give Ms Vuori some privacy.

"But this wasn't written by her father. Someone knew about their secret meeting spot. Someone knew their secret code." Wolflock glared at the note.

"How do you figure that?" the officer asked.

"Compare the two and tell me through pressure and style that you're smart enough to agree," Wolflock said with a bored drawl as he passed her a letter he'd taken earlier.

His mental web lit up before him with each thread of evidence sitting at a junction in the lines. In the centre was the child, Lija. The clues around her were her backpack, the lollies, some coated, some not, two receipts for her aunt's medicine, the letters from her father, the lines of strange code, and, finally, this last letter that did not fit with the others. That led him next to the people along this web. The mother, Ms Vuori, the father, Mr Dalur, Mrs Dalur, her aunt, and Saraesh. The places attached themselves to the clues and people associated with them. Lija's home and bedroom, the Växtadlare Apothecary, her aunt's home, these warehouses, her father's home, and the Guard Station. So many questions throbbed through his mind, each overlapping the last. There was just too much of this web to unveil still to draw any solid conclusions.

"This is a sticky mess." Mothy chuckled.

"So to Mr Dalur's house next?"

"No." Wolflock put everything back in Lija's backpack. "Next is the apothecary. Why would she have ordered two lots of medicine on the same day? There is something going on there, and there is more proof of Lija having gone there through the day, so they're more likely to have information on where she is now."

Rhiannon D. Elton

CHAPTER 5

Slugs & Vinegar

The evening chill followed their buggy through the twisting streets of Mystentine, with Theod's commentary announcing their incoming presence to every household they passed. The shaker-uppers walked through the streets, shaking the fairy dust lanterns before flying on their broomsticks to the next pole.

Wolflock grew frustrated that Theod only took them down main roads. He was convinced that, if he knew the map of Mystentine City better, he'd be able to whip them down a side road or cut across back lanes. He remembered looking at the maps of Plugh and dreaming of doing just that, racing away from the Thorn brothers and their wretched sister by dashing down an alley like a cat.

"Does the apothecary sell food? I'm a bit peckish. Is anyone else peckish?" Mothy asked Officer Tand and Ms Vuori.

"What time do you normally take supper?"

"Before bed, around three hours after sunset."

"Did Lija take food up to bed?"

"Yes. Some bread and cheese. But, she always did that. I thought it was just her getting hungry because she was growing still." Ms Vuori sniffled.

Wolflock rummaged in the backpack, but there was no trace of any food besides the lollies in it. She had thought she wouldn't have time to eat anything she'd taken, or she thought the trip would be short enough to not warrant snacks. Or, she assumed she would be fed at the other end of the journey. His hand stuck to the two types of lollies. Some were covered with a strange sugar and the others were smooth and pink. It was a gamble, but maybe something in them could lead them to where Lija was.

"Mothy, I need you to eat these lollies," he said, passing him the ones with the sugary coating.

"Now that's something I can do!" Mothy grinned

and began sucking on a candy.

Theod rounded a corner, and their destination came into view. The first thing he noticed about the apothecary was their hanging sign, embedded with silver, and the door that had quite beautiful silver leaves covering the nails. After being on the Silver Ice Hair for months, the presence of that metal made him feel quite at home.

Like everything else in Mystentine, it looked ancient. Wolflock jumped down from the buggy and raced to the door as he saw the upstairs lights dimming out. He pushed on the glass paned door, but it rattled against its lock. With a growl he grabbed the bell rope and rang it incessantly.

After a few moments, the sound of footsteps coming down old wooden stairs rumbled towards them. A brown shape moved behind the glass before the door opened with a click. A gaunt faced man with sharp golden eyes and thick caterpillar eyebrows stood before them with a thick book tucked under his pinstriped arm. His weary face opened the door as if he expected a dire emergency but evolved into confusion as none of the party looked injured.

"Merry meet. How can I assist?" he asked.

"I will need you to explain why you provided Lija

Vuori with two receipts for medication yesterday?" Wolflock flicked the two ribbons of paper at the man.

Mothy put a heavy hand on Wolflock's shoulder and began his sentence through a large yawn.

"Sorry 'bout that. What he means is that Lija has gone missing and-" he yawned again, "-Ms Vuori has asked us to investigate. We're just looking into every avenue so we can find her safe and sound."

Wolflock blinked at Mothy in surprise. He had no idea Mothy could act so professionally.

"Certainly, come in." The man stood to the side as he opened the door for them. "Kiipei, I'm so sorry to hear this. Let me know how I can help. Anything at all. Your nerves must be dashed. Officer Tand. Merry meet to you as well." He waved the three of them in and closed the door.

The entrance hall was repurposed to be a reception area with a small counter as the desk for receipts and paperwork. He started flicking through the papers until he found the original receipts.

"Was there a mistake, Dr Växtadlare?" Ms Vuori pleaded.

"You know that writing false receipts is a felony, doctor?" Officer Tand picked casually at her nails as he searched.

Both Wolflock and the apothecary looked at Officer Tand with contempt at the comment. Without a word, he returned to his searching, rolling his eyes. Wolflock developed an instant liking for the slender brown-haired apothecary.

"Here we are. She came in the morning and then went to her aunt's to deliver it. Not long after lunch, she came back saying her aunt had misplaced them. She didn't have money for the second lot, so I asked her to deliver the medicine to the children in the warehouse district as payment for the second lot. I do have to say, Ms Ingur Vuori does need to come in to be assessed for future medications. She can't keep self-diagnosing. It isn't safe."

"I... I'm sorry," Ms Vuori bowed her head.

"It's not your fault, Kiipei. Everyone knows she's been doctor hopping. I'm just letting you know, so she can't bully you into taking her to a new doctor again."

"Does this happen a lot? What was the medication for?" Wolflock asked as Dr Växtadlare drew them into a cushy lounge room. An adjoining kitchen sent rolling warmth into the heavily draped room. Each of them took a seat except for Officer Tand, who poked at the taxidermied creatures on the corner shelves.

"I'm sorry, I can't discuss patients' treatments with

members of the public. I maintain a strict patient practitioner confidentiality."

"It's fine, Heilari," Ms Vuori sighed. "My step sister always has lung problems and can't sleep because of her coughing,"

"What herbs did you give her?" Mothy opened his eyes to ask the question and then closed them again, propping his cheek up on his hand.

"It's all on her receipt. I make sure that the bag is clearly labelled and that the receipt also has all the details. I keep a copy here, too, just so my records are all straight." He looked pointedly at Officer Tand, who smiled in return. "Herbs for her nervous condition and cough. I have to source these from Chalongesh and Pyringel. They aren't particularly easy to get in a hurry, but they don't go off for months, so I try and keep a large supply."

"How strong are these herbs?" Wolflock asked, pinching his chin.

"They're all very strong. Not long after a dose most patients feel very relaxed and happy, and then they fall into a deep sleep for up to eight hours. I mean, there are always variables that change the response, but, generally, this is how it goes."

"Thank you. I think that's all we need."

Heilari turned to Ms Vuori and smiled sadly. "I'll get everyone out looking for her tomorrow. The students will be able to help our search efforts. We'll find her, Kiipei. We will."

The doctor knelt by Ms Vuori's armchair and took up the Antrum woman's hand with a tenderness Wolflock couldn't ignore. He shot a glance at Officer Tand, who raised a sharp eyebrow at him. She'd seen it, too.

"Have you noticed any strange substances circulating through Mystentine City lately?" Wolflock asked the doctor.

He patted Ms Vuori's hand and stood back up. Her hand clung to his for a bit too long as he rose. "What haven't I noticed? We've had an influx in toxic substances, causing terrible afflictions through the people. We often have an increase in vagrants coming into the city before Winter, but this year has felt far more extreme. The temples are bursting, and they can't handle the amount of charity they've had to deliver. They're running out of food, space to sleep, and clothing to give, as well as their own specialties, whatever they are. What's been worse is that many of the newcomers are violent."

"They're not normally?" Wolflock frowned.

"No. They're normally-"

"They just want a safe place to stay. Food, shelter, warmth, safe company. Most of them have problems we don't understand. They're not dangerous though," Officer Tand snapped.

Again, Dr Växtadlare and Wolflock shared a knowing glance.

"I understand that, Tand. I wasn't saying they are always dangerous. I'm just saying that the new ones have been. I believe that the increase in volatility is completely unnatural."

"Have you seen any traces of a refined purple powder?" Wolflock asked, annoyed that Officer Tand would get emotional about the topic.

Both Tand and Växtadlare stared at him with gobsmacked faces.

"How do you know about-"

"Why would you ask about-"

He smirked as they stumbled over their words, waiting for them to fall quiet before he answered. "I have been following its trail since not long after I got onto the Silver Ice Hair at Plugh. It seems to be causing all types of havoc, especially through this region, for about a year. Am I correct?"

Dr Växtadlare and Officer Tand looked hungry for the information Wolflock appeared to possess.

"Yes. Along with the increase in alcohol and other addictive chemicals, I've seen my fair share of people using a strange purple powder. The plant is ground down and processed in a way I haven't been able to reverse engineer. Those taking it seem completely without their wits, and follow every instruction with a drudge-like slowness," the doctor said.

"I've seen it used in gambling dens to make patrons give their every last sentus for another chance to win. What do you know about it?" Officer Tand stared at him with wide brown eyes.

"Well, I know a few things about it. It comes from a plant called the Lady Mind Master. The plant is dried, then ground down into a powder. The person distributing it is a cold, calculating man named Astraxis. He keeps a very controlling grip on those he hands it out to, and he's heading to Mystentine. I wouldn't be surprised to find that Mystentine has been his petrie dish to find out the side effects. I've seen it used on political officials, labourers, guardsfolk, witches, and even vampires. It's normally inhaled, but I came across a case where someone was feeding it to their victims, and it rendered them a mere shell of themselves."

His audience hung on his every word. Ms Vuori looked horrified.

"Is this... Did this Astraxis use this on my daughter?"

Wolflock shook his head. "There were no traces of it around the boxes where we found her bag. Also, I don't think he's in the city. At least, not yet. Our horse was much faster than anything he could summon, so we definitely beat him to Mystentine."

"This is going to destroy the city," Dr Växtadlare breathed, leaning back in his chair. Ms Vuori's hand flicked as if she were going to comfort him, but she kept it in her lap.

"Not so. We found a very clever witch who discovered an antidote."

"And preventative," Mothy mumbled from the armchair he'd curled up in.

The others waited for the answer, but Wolflock held his silence for just a moment more. "Wild lettuce."

Dr Växtadlare nodded slowly, then, as realisation spread over his features, his nodding sped up. "I see. I see." Everyone jumped as he gasped and flew from the room. "I have it!"

The slender doctor bolted like lightning and the others followed him into his pharmacy. Drawers filled the walls, floor to ceiling, with a long central table with sparkling glass equipment.

"It's part of the Solanaceae family, which means that mild opioids would degrade the receptors they fight over. Then you'd need something to eliminate the fatigue and clear the mind. Yes, yes, yes." The doctor threw his arms up and tore draws out of their shelves, stacking them in Wolflock and Officer Tand's arms. After he'd collected twenty-four different herbs, shells, and other minerals, he set to work with eyes ablaze.

Wolflock watched him, but he couldn't help seeing Ms Vuori smile serenely at him as he worked. She then caught herself and pain etched across her eyes again.

Dr Växtadlare ground one batch of ingredients into a powder, heated them over a Bunsen burner until they turned red, then gave the pestle and mortar to Officer Tand. "Stir this until I say stop. Get it as fine as you can."

"I'm not your lacky-" she protested angrily, but he had already turned back to his equipment.

Wolflock chuckled until the doctor passed him a bag of charcoal and white shells. "Smash this until it's powder and mixed. No chunks."

Mothy was asleep in the other room, otherwise Wolflock would have passed it on to him. The doctor mixed the minerals with a leafy mixture, then put the ingredients into different round beakers, steaming fluid through them until they flowed into a final tap. The doctor turned the nozzle, and a green and white pearlescent liquid dripped out.

"Huh..." Doctor Växtadlare leaned back, scrutinising his work. "No. That's not right. This powder doesn't match this one. Did you mix it thoroughly? It's meant to look like this."

The doctor scolded Officer Tand and plonked a small bag on the bench with a dark purple powder.

"Maybe this is what it looks like fresh?" Tand argued.

"No. No, I doubt it. There's only one ingredient I haven't been able to identify. That's the one that makes it purple."

Wolflock's mind sparked, and he flicked his journal open to the first few weeks he was on the Silver Ice Hair. "Would it be an animal ingredient? Something like this?" He drew out the handkerchief holding the dried purple pieces of the Sea Slug of Death Nü had identified after they saved the ship from the river bug poisoning.

Dr Växtadlare took the piece in his fingers and put it under a thick scope clamped to the table. He then broke pieces into different vials of clear liquids, but each turned different colours. "This is highly toxic. How did you get a hold of this? I doubt any medical person would use this in a medicine. This is purely lethal."

"Apparently, it's used by assassins in Xiayah."

"So we have a sea creature from Xiayah, a plant from Shellinden, more plants from Chalongesh, and roots from Ulusai'il. No wonder everyone is having trouble finding a solution for it. It's even less of a wonder that the cure comes from each of these locations as well. This ingredient though... Very strange." The doctor looked it over, thinking for a moment, before placing the chunk into Officer Tand's mix and setting it above the Bunsen burner again on a low heat.

The powder bubbled as if it were boiling, and each particle that moved turned into a perfect dark purple.

"Such a process to get this, and it's being used so flippantly. Whoever is distributing this is getting paid a lot, and whoever is paying them is expecting a lot out of this." Officer Tand scowled.

The doctor mixed a portion of the powders with a drop of his antidote, but nothing happened. The drop didn't even mix with the powder.

"Hmm..." he hummed, then stalked out of the room, returning moments later with a large bottle of vinegar. He mixed it with the test drops, and they turned white like salt, then dissolved. "Ladies and gentleman, we have it. The antidote for our problem."

"How do you know it works?" Officer Tand rolled her eyes. "And how am I supposed to know you didn't know how to make this all along and that this boy is your nefarious apprentice? I'm not stopping my investigation, Väx."

"Care to test it?" he gestured to the stool by the bench.

"And let you make a fool of me? No thanks."

"I'll test it," Wolflock spoke up. It was for science. There was no question he'd try it.

He put himself on the stool and waited expectantly.

The doctor's grin faded, but, with a shrug he positioned Wolflock with his arm on the bench to protect him from falling.

"Just close your eyes and breathe normally. This may prickle your nostrils. I'm going to tell you to drink the antidote. I need you to try and resist for as long as you can, yes? Tand, put this mask on and stand behind him. He might topple back if it makes him drowsy."

She masked up and stood behind Wolflock with her hands pressed on his shoulder blades. He did as he was told, curious about using the strange powder in a controlled environment. Closing his eyes, he waited, then heard the doctor puff. His face was filled with the sensation of having sand blasted at him, but it lasted far longer than he expected, prickling all the way down his face and neck. It wrapped around his head and his body felt numb.

"Drink the antidote," he heard the doctor's voice echo in front of him. The voice sounded like a warm crackling fire, and, as he opened his eyes, the doctor's face glowed like a beautiful fae. He ran his hand over the bench to his right and his hand hit the bottle. He wanted to drink it. The beautiful doctor told him to. It must be good. Fulfilling that command made his gut swirl with excitement. The doctor would be happy. He should drink it.

He didn't conceive a moment that he could resist.

He gulped the liquid in the bottle and his tongue burned from the intense, bitter taste. Just like the prickling from the powder had washed over him, the bitter burned it away. He felt like he'd dunked his face in a bucket of snow. His head and shoulders were drenched with sweat and he hadn't realised Officer Tand held him around his chest to keep him safe.

"Whoa there, genius. Steady now," she spoke in a calm, strong voice.

"Wha-what happened? Why am I wet?"

"Let me make us some tea while he recovers." Dr Växtadlare's sound returned to its normal husky low tones and his face stopped glowing.

Wolflock felt a powerful urge to stretch and writhe as he watched the doctor leave. Ms Vuori followed him.

"Are you brave or stupid?" Officer Tand chuckled, holding him steady while he moved. "Can you stand?"

"Let me try. That was bizarre. Have you ever tried that stuff? It's horrible," Wolflock groaned, sliding off the stool and to his feet.

"I have. I was about to bust a gang of kids injuring horses to steal from the occupants when the leader blew it in my face. They told me to walk to Creast. If it wasn't for Lija, I very well might have. She caught me and splashed me with some water. The effects lingered for a bit longer, but I could make my own choices again after that. How was the antidote?"

"Worse than the poison. It tastes like medicine and feels like cold fire over your skin. You've known Lija for a while, then?" He took slow deep breaths, feeling himself getting steadier.

"She was my trainee. I was helping her get ready to go into the Guard. She helped me get through to the other kids."

"How so?" Wolflock took another sip of the remaining antidote, thinking it was best to finish the bottle in case of any residual effects, and regretted it. The bitter taste made his spine quiver.

"Well, she said she got teased by one of the kids hanging out around her father's warehouses, and, when she stood up to them, she earned their respect. She joined their little gang and, one day, they got up to a bit too much mischief. She took the fall for all of them. I hauled her in for a night, but she wouldn't give up a single kid. Just kept saying it was all her and that she was insulted that I didn't think she could have pulled it off all by herself."

Wolflock chuckled. "That's loyalty."

"Sure is. I saw a lot of potential in her. She helped a lot of them get apprenticeships all over town. You know, learning practical skills and artistic skills to keep them out of trouble. With her influence, the inner city has basically no crimes committed by children."

"With child crimes down, why was there so much hubbub at the Guard Station?"

Officer Tand's lips pulled to the side as she hesitated. "It's all adults. Violence, gambling, theft, attacks from family members, and that's not to say anything about the health issues that have arisen over the last year. Until the next Ostara funding is released, we don't have the resources to do more. We also won't get new recruits until after the frost."

"Sounds like you're stuck between a rock and a hard place."

"Tell me about it. If the doctor's remedy works, though, we should be on the mend. I might even stop investigating him for it."

"He didn't do it. You're barking up an innocent tree." Wolflock wiped his face and neck down with the hand towel at the end of the bench.

"How do you know?"

"Will you believe me if I tell you?"

Officer Tand smirked. "You know, you're starting to grow on me. I might have to show you what's in that file tomorrow morning if you keep winning me over."

"Trust me," Wolflock scoffed, "it isn't like I'm trying. I just want to find Lija before anything happens to her. I can't get up to the university without her."

"Selfishly unselfish. What a puzzle. Now, tell me, why isn't it the doctor?"

"Firstly, he didn't have the ingredients to make it until I gave him the final one. Secondly, he has been far too busy. His dockets at the reception counter just for yesterday were numerous. That tells me he has students in to cope with the patient load. He'd have to supervise them and, unless he's convinced them that powder is something different, they'd become suspicious. And, thirdly, he's in love with Ms Vuori."

"It wasn't just me?" Officer Tand huffed happily. "I thought it was in my head."

"Of course not. Those prolonged hand touches, the amount of concern he expressed, addressing each other by their first names. I wouldn't be surprised if they come back in here and he makes her something to placate her sister, and something for her nerves."

"So you're saying he wouldn't have kidnapped Lija or put her in danger because he loves her mother? I'll believe that. What do you think happened?"

Wolflock examined his mental web and wondered where Officer Tand fit into all this. "I'm not sure. We need more data. I can't create a theory without more facts."

"Smart. I don't think it was her father. Bit of a poorly thought-out plot to steal your own child from your workplace, isn't it?"

"Possibly."

Their conversation ended as Ms Vuori and Dr Växtadlare came back in with fresh peppermint tea. They accepted their cups and Ms Vuori said they should head to her sister's. The doctor insisted on sending her off with something to calm her nerves and an extra bag to ingratiate her to her sister for the late visit.

Wolflock helped the snoring Mothy into the buggy. Officer Tand wished them a good night and hailed a new buggy.

"I'll see you both in the morning. Let me know what you find out at Ingur's house. Try to rest, Ms Vuori. We'll find her tomorrow. I can feel it. Merry part, Ms Vuori. Deputy Felen."

"Wait, what? Deputy?"

"Just until Lija is found."

They waved her merry part, but Wolflock thought it was a bit strange that she addressed Ms Vuori's sister in such a friendly manner.

CHAPTER 6

Secrets of the House

Wolflock held the sleepy Mothy on his seat as they drove to Kiipei's sister's home.

"Is there anything I need to know before we reach Ms Ingur's residence?"

The Antrum woman leaned back in the buggy and squirmed in her seat. "Well, she's not my sister. Not by blood. My mother remarried after my father passed away on the mountain. She married Ingur's father, but, because of the prestige of our name and bloodline, he made his daughter take our family name."

"And why is that relevant?"

"She's... a bit resentful. I also inherited the business and family home. My mother and stepfather both agreed that the house had too many stairs for her, and they knew I loved it much more than them."

"I sense that there is something else in this." Wolflock watched her closely in the pulsing streetlights.

"They knew I would help look after her if I had the larger income source. She hasn't been known to be giving, and they worried she'd hoard all the wealth for herself, and disgrace the name and business."

"And how do you look after her?"

"I pay for all her medicine, her handmaid, and I give her a percentage of the business for her to do with what she wants. She also receives a disability pension on top of the regular government income. I feel so guilty for not seeing her more often but, whenever I do see her, I feel like I've been drained of all my energy. My work also takes Lija and I away for a few days at a time, so that cuts into our visits."

"Disability pension?"

"Oh, yes. She's often chair-bound. She can only walk very short distances with great exertion."

Wolflock had a lot to ponder as they drove on.

It was well into the evening by the time they arrived

at Ms Ingur's abode. All the while, Wolflock sketched in his notebook, keeping a close eye on streets, street names and notable landmarks they passed. As the carriage stopped, Mothy jerked awake with a snort and a spasm that knocked Wolflock out of the buggy.

"Whassat?" he mumbled, blinking his eyes until he could focus. "Where are we? Why was I asleep?"

Wolflock let Ms Vuori explain as he looked around the street. Ingur's home was another townhouse that was well kept and thin, but stretched back enough to make sufficient space for three people to be comfortable.

Ms Vuori rang the bell at the door and, after a few moments, the handmaid, still wearing her day uniform, greeted them.

"Oh, thank goodness you've arrived! She's been coughing all afternoon. It's better than last week, but this cold snap is doing her no favours. I expected you earlier than this, though. Where is Lija? Who are these gents?" The maid spoke fast with a thick accent.

She was stocky, with blonde hair pulled back in a low bun and a pretty, caring face. At the mention of Lija, Ms Vuori burst into tears. Mothy took the bag of medicine from her and passed it to the handmaid.

"If you make these up for her, the cough might stop," he said as he soothed Ms Vuori, helping her inside.

Wolflock looked around the pristine entrance hall and analysed the sitting room Ms Vuori took them too. Before he could get a good look, he felt Mothy go past him. He heard his friend offer sleepy instructions to the handmaid in the kitchen at the end of the house. As Ms Vuori sniffled, Wolflock tried to comfort her, but his awkward shoulder pat felt entirely unnatural, and he doubted it was comforting.

They sat in the parlour, listening to the clicking noises of the kitchen as the handmaid prepared the decoction, as well as a forced, airy cough from upstairs. Mothy returned not long after, still looking drowsy. The three of them sat in an awkward silence for some time. Wolflock sat, elbows on knees, by the smouldering embers of the fireplace, lost in his web of thought.

After another half an hour, the coughing subsided, and the handmaid returned with a tray of biscuits and tea, looking tired and relieved.

"Thank you for waiting. Ms Kiipei, where is Lija?"

"She's-she's missing," Ms Vuori sniffled and dabbed her eyes. "These boys are helping me find her. Officer Tand will be back around in the morning to join us. You haven't seen her, have you, Gretah?"

The tray the handmaid held clattered to the table as it slipped from her hands.

"Officer... An officer? That sounds terribly official. Are you sure they should come here? I only saw her yesterday when she came to drop off Ms Ingur's medicine."

Wolflock sensed her lie. Something about her tone seemed too nervous. She didn't want an officer here. She was helping Ms Ingur get more medicine than she should safely have. Did she do something to Lija because she discovered what was going on? Or was there something else?

"Just the one time?" Wolflock asked, not looking away from the fire.

"I suppose so."

"You suppose so?"

"Well, it was a difficult day for Ms Ingur. I don't rightly remember who came and went by the house."

"Ms Ingur gets a lot of visitors?"

"Well... no... not so much."

"Were you here last night?"

Blinking in surprise, Gretah gripped her apron as she thought.

"I'm here every night. I live with Ms Ingur in order to look after her. I was here."

"What time did Lija come here yesterday?"

"Umm... Must have been around dusk. She came

with the normal medicine bags and took her bag of treats as usual. There was a problem with the medicine, so I had to send her back for more. When she didn't come back, I figured she was on one of her missions out late, but she didn't come all evening. Even if she arrives in the latest hour, she is normally quite dependable."

"Did she often come around very late?"

Ms Vuori looked up intently.

"Oh, aye. Sometimes with medicine and sometimes just for treats. She has a real sweet tooth, she does. Likes to talk about all the friends she has and her work at the Guard Station."

"Did you give her these?" Wolflock asked and showed her the bag of pink candy Mothy had been eating. He noticed that Mothy's eyes were hanging low. He nestled back into the chair comfortably.

"Nay. I don't make hard candies like this. I normally make her cakes and biscuits. This is probably from the Guard Office. They have these to help the kids be more comfortable."

"I wonder why Officer Tand didn't tell us that." Wolflock pinched his chin, leaning back into his chair.

Gretah smiled and let go of her apron. "If that will be all, I'll get your rooms ready. You are staying this evening, Ms Vuori?"

"Thank you, Gretah. Could we see my sister this evening by any chance? I don't know if I'll sleep without knowing my little girl is safe."

Gretah shook her head. "Of course, Ms. But the medicine knocks her out cold when she has it. Best chance for a chat is in the morning over breakfast, but you're welcome to see her. I'll go make those rooms for you all. This one," she gestured at Mothy, "is out cold, and you all look like you've had a big day. Wait here a moment and I'll be back shortly. Please, have the tea."

Gretah nearly ran from the room and Wolflock's eyes narrowed. Something was going on in this household and his suspicions wouldn't let him ignore it.

Ms Vuori followed her out and turned up the stairs.

"Wait here. I'll be right back," Wolflock said to the sleeping Mothy as he rose and followed Gretah down the long hall to the kitchen. He knew the letter telling Lija to go to the place she had last been seen was their best lead, but what if Gretah had been the one to write it on behalf of Ms Ingur? Why was she being so skittish?

The quaint kitchen of stone and iron was in pristine condition. Clean pots and pans hung everywhere, and the pantry displayed all manner of colourful fresh vegetables, still looking crisp and bright. Wolflock tucked himself behind the door frame as Gretah tore open the draw by the back door and hastily wrote something down. Her face looked panicked, and her movements were agitated and sharp. Did she know something that could help them? Why was she hiding it? Was she connected with Lija's disappearance?

As she folded the letter away and began to prepare the wax seal, he took action. He couldn't let her seal it before he'd read it. He knocked on the doorframe.

"Oh!" she cried and dropped the stick of red sealing wax.

"I was a bit lost. Where is the restroom?" he asked with a smile.

"J-just down the hall to the left. I was just getting the bedpans prepared," she breathed as she scooped up some flat pans and dashed past him.

Wolflock waited for her to get up the stairs before he slipped into the kitchen and flipped open the note.

Tand,

What have you done? Please tell me it wasn't you. Lija has gone missing. I need to hear it from you. Meet me at the fountain at Silfur Square as soon as you can. I'll be there all night.

Gretah

Flicking the note closed, Wolflock slipped back out and re-joined the sleeping Mothy. He'd finished the bag of lollies along with Ms Vuori, who looked as if she may finally nod off as well.

"Is your energy drained?" Wolflock asked with a smirk.

Ms Vuori sighed, "More than I thought it would be. She wasn't grateful about the medicine and, when I told her Lija was missing, she just groaned about having to pay her errand boy more now. I'm the one who pays her house staff."

"Did she say anything about Lija?"

Ms Vuori rolled one of the candies in her mouth, clinking it along her sharp teeth. "Only that she asked if she could stay here last night. That sounds odd to me."

"Do you think she's lying?"

"I don't know why she would. Perhaps Lija thought she could collect more of this information Officer Tand spoke to us about. I just feel like there is so much of my baby that I didn't know about. I don't know what to believe."

Wolflock scrunched up his face. "In my experience, your instincts. For some reason, there seems to be a part of your mind that sees things faster and puts them together more comprehensively than your conscious mind. You can't go wrong if your instincts say something is amiss."

"Good advice..." she yawned, "Ingur... will hate it... My instincts tell me she's always lying..."

Moments later he heard Gretah come down the stairs and head back into the kitchen. She gave her letter to the errand boy out the back and ran back to catch up on the time she'd lost getting her guests to bed.

"Your rooms are ready. Let me get you all tucked in with some tea and we'll help you look for Miss Lija first thing in the morning."

Wolflock helped Mothy upstairs and only took off his shoes before he got into the second single bed. As Gretah did her rounds, he pretended to fall asleep, listening for his moment to follow her. What did Tand have to do with Lija's disappearance?

Gretah tended to Ms Ingur first, then Ms Vuori, then checked on the boys before gathering some bits and pieces around the house. Finally, she doused the lights and locked the front door. Wolflock threw off his blankets, crammed on his shoes and dashed down the stairs. He flew through the back door, past the sleeping errand boy, and ran down the back alleyway, meeting the freezing cold street just as Gretah's dress flitted around the corner, heading further into town.

The air chilled Wolflock to the bone and regret for following Gretah without an overcoat hit him just as she stopped by the still fountain. She hopped from one foot to the other nervously. Wolflock circled around in the shadows, finding a spot to squat down behind a small set of stone stairs leading up to someone's townhouse. It was as close as he could get without being seen.

Just as the tips of his fingers began to lose feeling from the late Autumn evening, Gretah's lady arrived. The familiar, sturdy woman in a blue uniform strode over and folded her arms. Gretah rushed to her and rubbed Tand's upper arms anxiously.

"You got my note?"

"Well, obviously."

"Do you know anything? That poor little girl! I didn't want to get you in trouble, but we have to help! If you know anything-"

"Why would I know anything?" Tand snapped and shrugged her arms away.

For a moment, Gretah looked hurt, then she smiled sweetly and rummaged through her bag.

"You've had a bad night, haven't you?"

"No," Tand pouted, sniffing, and throwing her head back as her chestnut hair came loose from her bun.

Gretah chuckled. "Alright. Yes. I have had a bad night. The case I've been working on fell apart and I've been sidled with a brat I have to listen to for the sake of a client. He's not that bad but he pushed so hard we missed lunch. Chestir is being a pain as well. You'd think he'd get the hint."

"You can't blame him. To everyone else, you look single. And you're stunning. Let me get rid of those hangries. I brought your favourite."

Tand's stiff demeanour changed instantly as Gretah pulled a cloth bag of warm, cinnamon-smelling, baked treats. Wolflock took a deep breath and realised someone nearby had lit some kind of smoking herb nearby, as it tainted the sweet pastry smell.

"I had to make them myself today because I couldn't leave the house. I know they're not as good at bakers'."

Tand's face melted into a smile as the delicious cinnamon cookie crumbled in her mouth and she wrapped an arm around Gretah, keeping them both warm as Wolflock shivered behind the stone stairs.

"After she found us last night... how did you, you know? Deal with it?" Gretah flinched as she spoke the words.

Tand shuffled her weight around. "This isn't your

fault, understand? Lija was a curious little girl and it got her into trouble. You did nothing wrong."

"How can you say that when we're running around like criminals?" Gretah pleaded.

"You know if the captain found out there would be drama. I don't want everyone's noses in all our business. It's just so much simpler if we don't have to tell anyone. I like working in the inner city. I don't want to lose my cases or get transferred, because I love you." Tand took up Gretah's hands and gazed into her eyes.

"Her mother is at Ms Ingur's house. What am I meant to do, knowing she's missing, and we might be the cause of it? I thought dealing with it meant explaining to her that we had a secret, not making her go missing."

"I had nothing to do with that. Listen, Lija had a theory that street children were going missing. She thought something in the office had secret clues for it, so I showed it to her. Then, I walked her home. I didn't see her the entire day before I knew she went missing."

"If you told anyone you'd be in trouble from the captain, wouldn't you?" Gretah sighed, resting her head on Tand's chest.

"And what about you? You'd be in trouble too. I can't risk that."

"I'd be in more trouble if Ms Vuori found out Ms

Ingur was lying."

"Hmm?" Tand stroked Gretah's hair.

"She just wants her sister to stay longer. Little Miss Lija didn't stay at the house last night. I only saw her when she dropped off the medicine. Ms Ingur told me to send her to get more. I hate lying. She just wanted to be helpful. Ms Ingur wouldn't even let me give her the coin for it. Wanted it for free because it wasn't strong enough."

"I could put you with any other household you like, my love. Just say the word and you can have the nicest place to work."

"Oh I like my work, Tandy. I feel like I'm the last shield between Ms Ingur and the beautiful city we're in."

The couple swayed gently back and forth by the fountain. Wolflock couldn't feel his fingers anymore and his shoulders ached. He took a step further into the shadows, when Gretah exclaimed.

"Oh! I almost forgot. Mrs Dalur came around yesterday. She banged on the door so hard I thought she would break it. She thought her husband was there. Ingur was in an exceptionally good mood seeing her so upset."

"How did you get rid of her?" Tand frowned, looking down at Gretah.

"I told her they weren't in and invited her for tea. I think me inviting her in proved to her that they weren't there. I asked Lija what it could be about, but she didn't seem confused about it. She just said she needed to see her pa and left."

The conversation came to a halt when something moved in one of the streets leading away from the fountain square. Wolflock could see a figure moving in the darkness. Tall, thin, and scratching their head. The ladies hadn't seen them, but Wolflock saw them sit on a set of stairs and light a rolled smoke with a strange red glowing implement.

"I have to get back soon. I don't know anything about Miss Lija, but she only ever reported to Captain Estivan. He sent her out with me only occasionally on new crime scenes of the missing kids, where she couldn't get into trouble. I guess, sometimes, he'd get her to watch places like the urchins used to. Please, promise me you'll stay home, Gretah. We're trained professionals. We'll get this sorted. I don't want you to put yourself at risk."

"Like you do every day?" Gretah put out her bottom lip.

"Yes. My desk is terribly dangerous. All those sharp pens and paper cuts. Now, promise me." Tand took Gretah's chin between her fingers and lifted it gently.

"As long as you promise to stay safe, too."

Tand kissed Gretah and stepped back, puffing out

her chest to show the gleaming gold dragon crest.

"Trained professional, remember?"

They embraced once more and parted ways. For a few moments, Wolflock couldn't move due to the cold, but, as he cracked his muscles back into action, he realised that he had to beat Gretah home, otherwise she'd suspect something was wrong.

Racing down the dark cold streets with the chilly wind whipping through his hair, Wolflock's feet hit the cobblestone road, running. Remembering the lefts and rights back to the townhouse, he finally ducked down the alleyway and saw the back door. He opened the back door as quietly as he could and made it to the top of the stairs just as Gretah's key hit the front door. He kicked off his shoes and didn't bother removing any other clothes before slipping into bed and trying to cover as much of himself with the blanket as possible to get some feeling through his face. Gretah hummed gently as she locked up the rest of the house and came upstairs to bed, first checking on each room and her mistress.

It took Wolflock quite some time to settle down into sleep, but his dreams became his mental web, glowing with the fresh clues of tonight.

CHAPTER 7

Mr & Mrs Dalur

Wolflock tossed and turned all night as he slept on the clues before him. What had Officer Tand shown Lija? How did that tie in with her disappearance? Why was Captain Estivan keeping things secret from his own team? Why had Lija's stepmother come looking for her husband here?

The questions bounced around in his head. Every time he thought he came close to an answer, another question cut across it. He felt grateful to see the dawn light driving the shadows of night away on the other buildings he could see through the window.

He rolled over to see Mothy snoring in his peculiar sleep contortion act. Wolflock sat up and brushed his hair with his fingers. His toiletries were back at the Raven's Burrow Mountain Tours, and he didn't want to use anyone else's brush or comb, even if Gretah had laid them out on the dresser for him and Mothy. He tidied himself up and put his shoes on before clicking his fingers by Mothy's face. He just kept snoring.

"Mothy. Mothy wake up," he sang. Mothy snored louder in response.

With a smirk, he clapped his hands by Mothy's ear.

"Huh wha!?"

And instantly regretted his decision.

Mothy threw out his arms and legs like a scrambling deer, whacking Wolflock in the face twice and landing a heel to his gut, sending him reeling backwards onto his plush bed.

"Lockie?" Mothy slurred as he unwound his limbs from the blankets and sat on the edge of his bed. He scratched his fine, mousy hair and wiped his eyes. "S'wrong?"

"I wanted to tell you what I heard last night," coughed Wolflock. "Now I'm less inclined..." He rubbed his jaw as he looked daggers at his friend.

"Oh? I was bone tired last night. Couldn't keep my eyes open. What'dya find out?"

Wolflock told him of Gretah and Tand's exchange before the sound of a bell called them down to breakfast. Mothy pouted after he heard Wolflock had gone without him, but his mood changed when he saw the beautiful breakfast laid out for them across a dark wood table with individual green cushioned seats that matched the heavy green drapes. Fresh bread, boiled eggs, toasted seed muffins, porridge with dried fruit, and stewed root vegetables with salt and Northern spices tantalised them into their seats. The aromatic cacophony of smells made the boys' bellies rumble as they started piling their plates.

Mothy immediately started shovelling food, but Wolflock looked around to see where their host may be. Gretah pushed a delicate chair into the room with a frail, pale-looking woman who seemed nothing like Ms Vuori.

"Ms Ingur Vuori, I presume. It is a pleasure to finally meet our host."

He gave Mothy a kick under the table, so he'd display some manners.

"Thanks for letting us stay," Mothy smiled through a mouth full of bread.

Ms Ingur eyed them from her emaciated sockets. Her thin form was shawled in a dark black wool blanket and her brittle, decorated fingers wrapped around a ceramic cup like a heavily jewelled crow's foot.

"Please forgive my lady but her coughing fit yesterday as left her without a voice," Gretah soothed, and poured them all some fresh spiced tea.

"Where is Ms Vuori?" Wolflock asked as he watched the strange, spindly figure move towards the porridge like a praying mantis.

"She said she wasn't hungry, so she's just writing in the study to get the word out about Miss Lija's disappearance."

"She'd better come back soon," Ms Ingur rasped as she prepared her spoon full of porridge, her opulent rings clinking on the metal. "Who else will bring my medicine?"

Gretah pressed her lips tightly together for a moment and they sat in an awkward silence.

"Ms Ingur, she didn't run away. She's gone missing."

Ms Ingur hissed. "Oh tosh. She's just at her father's, hiding away. Insolent child won't even care for her poor sick aunt. But that's what you get from an Antrum. No Yule presents for her this year. Her mother is no better-"

"Oh!" Gretah gasped, fishing a note from her

pocket. "I forgot to give you this. It was delivered this morning from Officer Tand. Oh, Ms Vuori!"

The poor handmaid squeaked as the Antrum woman dragged her feet into the dining room and took a seat midway between her stepsister and the boys. Her bloodshot crimson eyes looked up at Gretah with a weary sadness.

"Did you say they've sent word?"

"Umm... yes, ma'am. Officer Tand and Captain Estivan have set off for Mr Dalur's abode. They say not to worry about following until they have more information," Gretah recited for the room.

Wolflock thought she was being quite foolish. Ms Vuori had to unseal the note, which meant that Gretah shouldn't have been able to read it yet, and she had sealed it with a stamp and wax from the back postage room. He thought about highlighting it, but he didn't want to reveal her and Officer Tand without something to gain from it.

"We have to go. Have you got your things?" Ms Vuori jumped up, inhaling a muffin and apple juice from the table as she looked at the boys.

Wolflock nodded and drained the rest of his soup, but Ms Ingur wailed and fell back into her seat. All eyes turned to the woman as Gretah rushed to her side, but she continued moaning as if she were in great pain.

Wolflock watched Ms Vuori's face. With each wail her steely resolve chipped down until she bit her lips

"Ingur? What's the matter?" she asked the obligatory question.

"Oh, no. It's just that I hurt all over, dear sister. The doctor only gave you a half dose of the medicine, I'm sure."

She groaned again as the others looked on. Wolflock could have sworn he saw her smirk.

After a few tense moments, Ms Vuori asked, "What would you like me to do about that?"

Ms Ingur's thin lips curled in snarl. "I don't want you to do anything about it! I just want to sit here in agony and wait for the darkness to take me."

"Ingy, my daughter is missing-"

"Don't 'Ingy' me! This is just an excuse you've made up, so you won't have to see me. How long will she be 'missing' for, huh? A week? A month? All Winter? I'll just have to wait for medication, will I?"

Ms Vuori's lip quivered, but Wolflock had had enough.

"I mean you can always use the duplicates we have extra receipts for. Or ask your maid to collect them. Ah, but that won't do, will it, Ms Ingur?"

The crotchety woman's lip curled in disgust as

Wolflock spoke.

"No, of course not. You're after all of your stepsister's undivided attention in order to bring her life down to the state yours is in. You hide your medication and your addiction while doctor hopping to get a new pity party wherever you go. The worse off you make yourself, the more attention she has to provide your imagined ills without realising that it's due to her love of her work that you're able to afford any of this in the first place. Well, I'm terribly sorry, but we have to tend to real problems and we're in a rush."

"Ingy? Is that true? We saw the two receipts at Dr Växtadlare's. Is it true you've been spending our time on things you didn't need?" Ms Vuori breathed.

Ms Ingur writhed in her seat like a naughty child caught stealing candy. "Get out. You don't love me. You never do anything for me. I hate you."

Ms Vuori walked by her sister and looked down on her with terrible pity. "I love you. Because I love you, I won't feed this. I'm going to find my daughter." And, with that, she flew from the room.

"And we're done," Wolflock grinned as he rose from the table, only having half finished his bowl of soup. "Gretah, please help us with our departure. We must away to the Dalurs with great haste."

Ms Ingur blinked, unable to stammer out an argument as Wolflock grabbed Mothy by the shirt collar and hauled him out after Gretah, who smiled as she left the room. Mothy scooped up a napkin of breakfast muffins and waved as he was dragged away.

"Is she always that awful?" Wolflock asked as they caught up to her.

"Only when she's ill," the handmaid whispered.

"When is she well?"

She didn't answer.

"She'll regret her words if Lija is found in a poor state."

Gretah pressed her lips again. "Ms Vuori hasn't sent gifts to her family for more than five years now."

"She really doesn't like her sister and niece that much?" Wolflock asked as they came to the front door.

"She resents their good health and fortune. She thinks it's because of their heritage that they somehow stole it from her." Gretah whispered. "She's the only person in town who does though. Please find Miss Lija. I'm terribly worried about her."

"I'm sure we will. Lockie is the best finder of lost things I know," said Mothy through a mouthful of muffin.

As they walked into the early morning air, they saw Ms Vuori give a stack of letters to the errand boy who had brought Theod around for them.

"We're ready to go."

"Good, good. I'll take you to Uskoton's." She gave one resolute nod before stepping into the buggy and gripping the seat rail with white knuckles.

She's either nervous or outraged, Wolflock thought as he followed Mothy up.

"Did you sleep well, Theod?"

The little horse whinnied as he kicked off at a trot. "Oh yes, Mr Mothy. The other ponies in the stable work for the neighbours, and we stayed up all night talking. It was delightful."

Wolflock smirked to himself, thinking that, if the other horses complained, it would all come back to Ingur.

The Dalur's manor house was nestled away in the blocks at the base of the mountain to the West. Perfectly manicured gardens and flowerbeds surrounded the house, unlike the majority of other houses and townhouses, which had the occasional tree planted along the path surrounded by decorative fencing. The excessive attendants to a wealthy household was something Wolflock could identify very quickly. A good dozen staff trapezed like a line of ants down the path from the Dalur residence. Servants carried all kinds of boxes and blanket wrapped trinkets, loading them on to wagons.

"What's going on?" Wolflock frowned at Ms Vuori.

"I can see why she snuck over here to see her father," Mothy said as he helped Ms Vuori down from the carriage. "This place looks like a lot of fun for a child."

Ms Vuori heaved a sigh. "He'd have you believe it was my selfishness that stopped Lija from being able to come here. I may have loved him dearly, and I was terribly mad at him, but I did it for her safety. Mrs Dalur hates both of us and I needed to protect my daughter. When I confronted his wife about it, she said that it was the duty of a parent to discipline children. I would never strike Lija. She's a clever and trusting child because of that. She's utterly fearless. She knows she can trust me to talk to her about what is right and wrong, and striking someone else is always wrong! Especially someone smaller than you."

Wolflock didn't know if he agreed with her or not, but Mothy nodded along as if her teachings were wise, so there had to be some merit to them. He stepped out of the buggy and walked down the long driveway as Mothy helped Ms Vuori down.

On the white stone front porch stood a finely dressed, thin woman with lines around her lips that made her mouth look like a drawn purse. Her dusty brown hair was swept back into a loose bun decorated with pearls and her long black dress frilled around her thin long neck.

At first, Wolflock noticed that she looked over the workers carrying out boxes and furniture with a smile of relief, but, as she saw the three of them approaching, her lips pulled in like drawstrings and she looked down her hooked nose with hooded eyes.

"Mrs Dalur, I presume," Wolflock jogged to the top of the stairs ahead of them and bowed politely. As he drew nearer, he smelt a familiar flowery smell.

She sniffed stiffly. "That is correct."

"Pleasure to meet you. I'm Councillor Felen. We're here for a meeting with yourself, Mr Dalur, and my client, Ms Vuori. I believe we are on time."

Mrs Dalur's nose twitched, and she refused to look at Ms Vuori. Mothy and Ms Vuori blinked at Wolflock in surprise, but they stayed silent and let him lead.

"I... But... I wasn't inform- I mean, of course I knew about this meeting. Let me show you to the parlour."

Wolflock smiled and let her show them to what would have once been a beautifully decorated room, but was now covered in white cloth and marks from where the old paintings had been taken off the wall.

"I'll fetch Mr Dalur. Please wait here."

They took seats on the covered sofas and felt the dry warmth from the fireplace. Wolflock glanced into it and noticed a crumpled page sitting just out of the heat by the back wall. He took up the tongs and fished it out before it could burn anymore.

Dear Kiipei

I hope this finds you and Lija in a better mood. I have had an upheaval of the home and I will send this letter with some house staff to help look for Lija until I can be there.

Yours Always,

Uskoton

Wolflock grinned, thrusting the note in front of Ms Vuori and Mothy.

"I've always wanted to impersonate a lawyer before," he said as he smiled ear to ear.

"I'm all for a bit of sneaking and mischief, but why didn't you count me in?" Mothy asked.

"I could see as we walked up the stairs that she was going to have us thrown out, but Mrs Dalur is an arrogant woman. From what I'd heard of her, and how she conducts herself, she wouldn't have wanted the household and staff to know that her husband had not kept her informed of the goings on. But it was not such a far-fetched story that he would do such a thing, as we've seen by his dishonesty to his wife, mother of his child, and business partner. So, she was forced to play along to save face, especially in front of the woman who she feels not only stole the heart of her husband, but also had a child with him. She doesn't have any children, does she?"

Wolflock spoke as he casually examined the items left in the room. The mantel had been cleared, as had the shelves and drawers, but a small porcelain container of hand cream sat next to one of the armchairs. He opened it and sniffed it. Chamomile, comfrey, and lavender honey. He recognised the blend from the Arain province in West Grothener.

"Not that I know of, but why does that even matter? People are allowed to adopt and have surrogate children. Isn't that encouraged where you come from? It certainly is here in Mystentine," Ms Vuori hissed in a whisper.

"I believe it may be part of her Troston upbringing. They believe that the worth of a woman is in her appearance, her ability to produce male offspring and her subservience to the men in her life."

Mothy nodded solemnly but Ms Vuori looked horrified.

"I never knew. I just thought she was bitter and hated me for her husband's sake."

"Kiipei!"

A tall gentleman with a short cut beard appeared at the door. Ms Vuori looked up and got to her feet, hands clutched at her chest. The man rushed in breathlessly, taking Ms Vuori's hands.

"Tell me you have news! I was going to join you and the others shortly, but things have been so busy here and I knew Silluvun would-"

"Stop. Stop." Ms Vuori gripped his hands back. "What are you talking about?"

"I... I sent Silluvun and the others to help you search. They've been gone for the last two days. You told me you were all looking high and low for her."

"You haven't sent me anything. Or anyone. These two boys and the locals are all who have helped."

"But my staff haven't been here for days! They must have been with you!"

"You're not making any sense. Now sit down and answer these boys' questions." Ms Vuori pulled her hands out of his and folded her arms tightly as Mr Dalur sat down, looking crestfallen.

Mrs Dalur returned and lurked at the door.

"Sir, where were you the night before last?" Wolflock began.

"Who are these boys, Kiipei? Why have you brought them here? We're wasting time not looking for Lija," he protested.

Ms Vuori looked him dead in the eye. "Answer the question, Uskoton."

"I was here with Ameiloe." He nodded to his wife, who kept glancing through the windows to the front gate. "We... We had a lot to talk about."

Ms Vuori eyed him with suspicion, but she stayed silent.

Her silence was enough to make him sweat. "It was... I just... She..."

"She? She! I'm your wife!" Mrs Dalur fumed, stomping away. As she disappeared from view, she screamed.

Wolflock could tell it was one of the utmost frustration, but Mr Dalur ran to the distress call. What Wolflock didn't expect was to hear other voices mingling with the calamity in the entrance hall. The boys raced from the room to see Captain Estivan grappling with Mr Dalur and Officer Tand standing between the couple. Even Chestir was with them, scribbling notes on a clipboard. He had jumped back, holding the clipboard up as a shield under his thick glasses.

"Stay back, boys." Officer Tand threw her hand out to stop them.

"Why are you restraining him?" Wolflock pointed at Captain Estivan.

"We heard a woman scream and saw her running." Tand gestured between them.

For a moment Wolflock saw relief cross Mrs Dalur's face again, but he didn't like that seeing her husband apprehended made her pleased.

"I think you'll find she screamed before her husband entered the room. Captain Estivan, what brings you here?"

He let go of Mr Dalur, who indignantly straightened his suit jacket and waited for the explanation.

"New evidence has come to light that Miss Lija's disappearance is directly related to your estate, Mr Dalur. We'll need you to cease your departure until we've conducted our investigation of your premises."

"Wait, what?" Mr Dalur and Wolflock said simultaneously.

Mrs Dalur gasped, falling to her knees.

"What departure?" Ms Vuori trembled in the doorway.

"If you two and Ms Vuori wish to stay and discuss matters with the Dalurs, be my guest, but stay out of the way of my team."

Five blue clad Guards marched in and, as Captain Estivan designated tasks to them, Wolflock grabbed Mothy's arm and brought him into a huddle with Ms Vuori.

"Mrs Dalur is hiding something. There is evidence here that we need, and that this rabble are going to miss."

"Oh, I don't know about that." Mothy looked over the troop. "They look capable to me."

"Mothy, they're rookies. They're still wearing training bands on their arms. They don't know what they're supposed to be looking for."

"And we're not rookies," Mothy grinned.

"Exactly. We need to be able to search the house without the Dalurs interfering. Ms Vuori, can you create a long enough distraction for us? We'll give you a signal when we've found what we need."

"Do you think Lija is here?" she spoke with a severe note in her voice.

Wolflock shook his head imperceptibly to the rest of the room. "I do not know. I know that there is more at play here than we first realised. Give us time and we'll give you answers."

With a resolute nod, Ms Vuori rose to her average height with the commanding energy of someone thrice her size.

"Uskoton, what do they mean by 'departure'?"

Mr Dalur paled, leaving Mrs Dalur on the floor as he moved to soothe the mother of his child. "It's nothing. Nothing at all to be worried about. I wasn't going to leave until we found Lija-"

"You said we were leaving tonight!" spat Mrs Dalur.

"Tonight?" shrieked Ms Vuori. "While our child is missing?"

"No-no, I-your-you see..." he stammered.

As Wolflock and Mothy slunk away to the stairs going up to the private rooms, he saw Mr Dalur for the man he really was. A complete, flip-flopping, people pleaser to the utmost degree. His desperation and boredom likely led him into the arms of many partners, but the two who could hold sway over him were the two who had a lifelong bond. Marriage and child.

It gave Wolflock a chill to think someone could be so mercilessly attached to another human. It certainly wasn't for him.

"Now," Mothy grinned as they found themselves in a cloth covered hallway, "we're not rookies, so we know what we're looking for. But, just so we're on the same page, what are we looking for?"

Wolflock smirked. "If the behaviour from downstairs is anything to go by, we're looking for Mrs Dalur's luggage that she intends to carry on her person, or a very special looking trunk. Something you'd put evidence in that could destroy your life but also gives you life. Perhaps something that hints to a family member, a religious leader or a secret lover."

"How do you figure that?" Mothy asked as he started flicking through the books left on a shelf in the study.

"She is set on leaving town. She also looked happy when her husband was being apprehended. She's not the smartest of women, but she's cunning. She has reasons for leaving town in a hurry and I doubt it's because she's hiding Lija anywhere here. She wants to get away from everything about her husband."

"Ah. You know, it's a typical Troston thing for the women to not be able to do anything without their husbands' permission. If he was locked up, he wouldn't be able to delay her leaving. She must really dislike him."

"Why the sudden need to leave though?" Wolflock scanned the white room as he looked for anything inconspicuous and personal. "They had discussed it on the evening Lija disappeared. No doubt we'll find the house staff can all confirm they were here." Suddenly the image of Lija sitting on the crates in the warehouse on the night of her disappearance was altered in his mind. Saraesh hadn't seen Mr Dalur talking with his daughter. She'd seen another man talking to her. To sit close enough to be comfortable with the person wasn't something a smart child would do with a stranger. She knew them. Lija knew the person who abducted her. But how could they have done it without alerting Saraesh?

Wolflock moved into the master bedroom and saw two piles of the luggage being kept aside for the Dalurs personal carriage. "Mothy, come and help me look through these, would you?"

"Oh, excellent. You found them. Good investigating, Lockie. You'll be two steps above a rookie in no time," Mothy chuckled as he began sifting through Mr Dalur's items. "He sure loves his daughter. Pictures, paintings, her sketches. It looks like he kept everything she ever made. I wonder, though..."

Wolflock opened Mrs Dalur's boxes and suitcases, finding masses of plain jewellery, bland clothes, and the entire set of the Troston bibles along with various prayer books. "What are you wondering?"

"What is in between a rookie and a master? You

always hear about being one or the other. But what is in the middle of all that? You don't just wake up one day after being a rookie for years and suddenly, 'poof', master."

"You can be an apprentice, a journey folk, an adept, an expert-"

Mothy laughed. "Ah. Hazzim always said to watch out for experts. They're not just a drip under pressure."

Wolflock gave him a short laugh out of courtesy, not really understanding, but his eyes were fixed on the lid of the suitcase he'd opened. There was less space in it than the outside suggested, but he couldn't see how the wooden underside could be altered.

"Huh... a secret compartment."

"I didn't know that was a level. I can't wait to reach 'secret compartment' level."

"Mothy, come look at this. What do you make of it? Does it look like anything you've seen before?"

Mothy ran across the room and came to a halt before the suitcase, skidding on his knees over the carpet. "What have you got for me?"

He ran his fingers all over the case, trying to cram his short nails into the edges and tugging on the belts glued to the inside like the ribs of a ship. "Oh? What's this? Lockie, look! It's that funny writing."

Wolflock saw Mothy pull down the tag for the company who crafted the case and, underneath, was another Corlesian pictograph code. After a few moments of deciphering it, Wolflock spoke words that made Mothy grip his shirt reflexively.

"In the name of our one Lord and Saviour, may my sins be only His to judge and may my soul follow his path. For His light is the only light in which we may eternally follow." Wolflock made a face of disgust. "It sounds like a warped prayer from the Temple of Light."

"Yeah... but the Temple of Light don't stone you to death if you walk in the darkness. They also don't dictate what darkness is to the point where you're walking on a tightrope that keeps moving." Mothy kept his grip on Wolflock's shirt.

"It has a spot at the end of it that's blank. What's that word the Trostons use in their prayers?"

Mothy shrank back, his face darkening with disgust. *"Ahlwanye."*

Wolflock jerked his hand away as the code burned red hot and the lid of the case sprung open with tiny sparks.

"Knock, knock, little deputies," came a soft voice from the door. Chestir knocked and slipped into the room, smiling nervously.

Both boys sat up like rabbits, alert with wide eyes.

"Oh, don't mind me. I just didn't want to... you know. The ladies. Oof, am I right?" he laughed. Neither of the boys returned his awkward joke. "Did you find anything? Goodness knows the captain is pulling at straws, ahah."

"I'm not sure, yet. But maybe."

"Oh, well, perhaps I can help a bit?"

Wolflock frowned, sensing Chestir's brittle energy and the stench of tobacco. It had the kind of interfering incompetence that required twice as much effort to negate than if it hadn't been there at all.

"Sure. The more help the faster we can find Lija." Mothy smiled at the lanky man.

Wolflock scrunched up his face in distaste, giving Mothy a clear signal that he was responsible for the incompetent clerk.

"This is exciting," the older man tittered, rubbing his hands together. "It's like real detective work."

"It is real detective work," Wolflock snipped.

"Oh, yes. Of course. Forgive me." Chestir raised his hands in apology and bowed his head. Wolflock noticed, for the first time, how thick his hair was. The chestnut strands that bobbed around his face and ears were as thick as Theod's mane.

Not wanting to give the man any more attention, he turned to the now open suitcase. Bundles of envelopes lay scattered in the top of the case, as well as bejewelled necklaces, men's rings and a portrait of a tall, thin, dark-haired man holding a happy Mrs Dalur. The surrounding image showed an orange lit stone church with other couples in modest dress. The mountain through the tall, thin window suggested they were in Mystentine when it was painted. The artist's name in the lower right corner stood out in white paint: Vicar Gorj T.T. Maroskov

The amount of detail in the small painting was phenomenal. Every tiny inch felt saturated with the care and delicacy of a professional, but the shape of the people in the background overpowered the couple in the foreground. Wolflock also noticed that Ms Dalur was the only feminine-looking woman. All of the others were painted to be misshapen, yet the men were glowing with power and radiance.

"Not very well hidden, was it?" Chestir laughed, as if he had been the one to discover it.

"No," Wolflock grumbled as he positioned the frame on its corner and pushed. "We're just smarter."

He squashed it, cracking the wood out of the nails enough to take out the painting and examine the back. Mothy took in a sharp breath as he watched Wolflock destroy property, but didn't say a word as his friend showed him the back.

"*Exactly as you asked, Lady Dalur. May yours and Eric's sins be safe with me as mine are with you. Gorj.*"

"A tall, dark haired, thin man," Mothy stared at the picture, but refused to touch it. "Do you think Mrs Dalur wanted to get rid of her stepdaughter?"

"Oh no," Chestir shook his head as he fiddled with the broken parts of the frame. "Mrs Dalur is a very polite woman. I don't think she has a bad bone in her body."

"Know her well, do you?" Wolflock rolled his eyes.

"Oh, no, not really. I just know of her. She's very charitable, and Mr Dalur hasn't been such a problem for the local ladies since she's been in town."

"Charitable to the local Troston church." Wolflock rolled up the painting and put it in his pocket. "Let's see if she did want to rid herself of Lija, shall we?"

He dug through the bundles of letters and the scattered notes for more information. The letters were all addressed to "my light" and "my love", with one stack from her sister in Corl.

"Look at this." Wolflock stacked the letters in front of Mothy. "For every letter he sent her, she wrote three or four back. They're all the same words, but they look like three different people's handwriting. She's been practising forgery."

"Forgery! Well, I never!" Chestir gasped, picking up the letters and turning them this way and that.

Mothy nodded, impressed. "Who has she been forging?"

"We have letters from who I can assume is Eric, the dark-haired man in the painting. He encourages her to write in Mr Dalur's hand, Ms Vuori's and Lija's. She even has a couple in Miss Ingur's hand."

He pulled out another letter in a new hand that read,

Dearest Mrs Dalur,

I wish to thank you for procuring your husband's generous contribution to our church. I hope , now you have his heart in your hand, that you will secure its regularity and we will prosper in the name of the one true Lord. You may now sit in the second pew. Please dismiss my previous urgings to bring Mr Dalur into our flock. I see, now, that his vicarious worship through you is sufficient.

In regard to your questions about annulment, I cannot perform such a sanction here. I beseech you that a loveless marriage is far greater in the eyes of our Lord than a second one, for that second betrothal will always be seen as a betrayal to the first. In your case, though, I can say that, due to the nature of your incompatibility with your husband, to produce a son and his lack of faith, I will ask you to pray on it and send my recommendation to Corl.

Please seek the word of the Wise and Mighty Lord through prayers with Vicar Gorj about his desired course for you.

Ahlwanye,
Father Jymes

"Wait..." Mothy frowned as he read over Wolflock's shoulder. "What is 'annulment', and did he give his blessing for it or not?"

Wolflock sneered. "It means she wanted to get a priest to say her marriage with Mr Dalur never happened and wasn't real. The funny thing is, the priest didn't want to have her annul it because she's been using Dalur's money to fund the church. This dark-haired man doesn't have the same level of wealth as her current husband. Greedy monsters. See if you can find the most recent responses from the dark-haired man."

They sifted through the letters with swift hands, adding to the piles of Mrs Dalur's responses in her own hand, in other people's hand, and the letters she received. Mothy realised the task he'd given himself as Chestir constantly put letters in the wrong piles and tried to grab them from the suitcase to help. He was irritatingly immune to Wolflock's death stare and continued to snatch up envelopes. He even put them back in the wrong envelopes. It soon became a competition between the two of them to see who could go through the letters faster.

"Best keep up the pace. Those ladies might finish their row any moment now."

Mothy accepted the charge of correcting Chestir's mistakes as he was the one to welcome him to their investigation.

Wolflock snorted. "Yes. Any moment now."

Chestir stopped his paper onslaught and cocked his head to the side with a wry smile. "Did you do something to rile them up?"

"Aha!" Wolflock found a letter dated the day before Lija's disappearance.

Mothy continued to fix his pile of papers before lifting another letter and flicking it open with the exact same "Aha!". After glancing at it, his jaw dropped. "Oh my gosh it is."

"Is what?"

"I was just making fun of you but this one is dated

the same."

Chestir cocked his head the other way, his smile flattening, "Is this all detective work is? Looking at papers and exclaiming?"

"Two letters sent in a day. Now that is curious. And risky." Wolflock flattened his on the floor as he sat next to Mothy.

To my love,

I can bear it no longer. Our Almighty has set a task between us that is too powerful for me. My only wish is to maintain your honour, but I cannot deny my passion for you anymore. Therefore, with the grace of our priest, I beseech you: Run to Corl and annul your marriage with your husband. I know you have been discussing it with Father Jymes. I will meet you there the very next day and we shall be blessed with dozens of beautiful sons as the Lord wishes it.

Please respond with all haste. I am packed and ready to follow you at a moment. I cannot bear another Winter without you in my bed.

Your true love.

The letter was unsigned. In fact, none of the letters in that hand were signed. The handwriting remained calm and controlled, standing in neat, parallel lines with the slightest hint of a right-hand slope. He then read the second correspondence she had that day.

My love,

I cannot delay. I will leave tomorrow with or without you. If I don't find you in Corl, I'll know your answer. You cannot use the disruption the child brings as an excuse. If you do not love me, say and I will be done. Why not send the child to the meeting spot she finds your husband at every night he is not home? That will give you the time you need to convince him to go to Corl.

My love for you will not allow me to delay this any longer. I hope, with all my heart, I will see you in Corl.

Your true love

"Really upped the pressure, didn't he?" Mothy scoffed.

Chestir leaned over, craning his neck to read them as well, but Wolflock folded them and moved to put them in his breast pocket.

"Umm... I don't mean to be a stickler for regulation, but... uh... shouldn't I keep hold of those? As evidence?"

"Ha. No." Wolflock looked him up and down, making a point of tucking the notes further into his pocket.

"I'll just make a note of that and let the captain know you're holding the evidence."

Wolflock leaned forward with a sneer. "Good." He then leaned back and turned to Mothy with a pleasant demeanour. "In answer to your question, Mothy, yes. He did put the pressure on her. She took the bait. She's convinced Mr Dalur to leave, and I doubt he even knows why. This tall, dark-haired man from the picture has been wooing Mrs Dalur for years. Now, all of a sudden, he's demanding she leave and annul her marriage in a city far away at the same time her stepdaughter goes missing and crime is on the rise in Mystentine."

Wolflock pinched his chin in thought as Mothy shuffled the letters in neat stacks. "Mothy! That's it!" Wolflock snapped his fingers. "Lija discovered the evidence she needed to find the other missing children in Captain Estivan's closed off room. The dark-haired man was the same one that took Ms Vuori's statement, and he made sure it was tucked into mountains of filing. She gave her statement to the man who orchestrated all of this. She saw the man who kidnapped her daughter!"

The boys sat for a few silent moments with the revelation. It made sense. But who was it? Mrs Dalur would know.

"Wowser! What a thrill. Here I was thinking Ms Vuori made the whole thing up to get us to hustle. There's no proof of much of this, though, is there? I mean, it's not like Captain Estivan has been really withholding that kind of information from us. He trusts his staff implicitly."

The boys knew that wasn't true. Captain Estivan hadn't let Officer Tand know anything and she had to sneak Lija in to get any clues at all. They both took off at the same time, grabbing the damning piles of letters and ran down the stairs, leaving Chestir alone in the room.

"We have it!" he cried as he ran down the stairs. Mothy slid down the bannister and beat him to the ground.

"Have what?" Captain Estivan snapped. The women either side of him were spitting and hissing like vipers either side of him.

"Mrs Dalur knows where Lija is!" Mothy blurted out before Wolflock could say anything.

The room fell into a stunned silence and Wolflock grinned at his own genius. He gestured to the parlour.

"Ladies and gentlemen if you don't mind taking a seat? This won't take long."

"This is not the time for games, boy," Captain Estivan growled, standing by the door with Officer Tand.

"Mothy and I have discovered the truth. Mrs Dalur, if you would like to come clean, you will save me an explanation."

"I don't know where the," she paused as if the word revulsed her, "child is."

"No, but you know who has her. Excellent. I was hoping you wouldn't take the fun of explaining what occurred. Well," he put his nose in the air and paced with his hands behind his back the same way he'd seen lawyers do, "over a decade ago, Mr Dalur married the now Mrs Dalur in Corl. He then moved to Mystentine to start a business, but relationships with his wife and her family must have been growing tense, otherwise, he would have brought her with him. Ms Vuori conducted a relationship with him, believing him to be unattached which led to the child Lija, being born.

"Upon hearing of this affair and receiving Mr Dalur's refusal to return to Corl, Mrs Dalur brought herself to Mystentine in order to attempt to restore her honour. This also forced his hand, and he had to confess his crimes of the heart to both parties, only being able to keep the one who felt obligated to remain with him through religious and legal practices. I'm correct, thus far?"

"You forgot he told Ms Vuori all this on her birthday," Mothy snorted.

Ms Vuori and Mrs Dalur both directed their seething rage at Mr Dalur, who shrank back at the weight of his misdealings. Chestir trotted down the stairs with his arms full of the envelopes they'd sorted. He stopped outside the door, listening with an ignorant grin.

"Lija had recently been forbidden to visit this home due to Mrs Dalur injuring her, which was not the practice for raising children in the Vuori family."

"You did what?" Mr Dalur gasped, looking up from his shoes. Chestir made a silent whistle and beelined for the front door.

"You speak as if you didn't know. How else was one meant to rein in such a wilful girl?" she hissed, making him return his gaze back to his shoes.

"You don't," was all Ms Vuori said, silencing the room.

"But the love of a parent and child is powerful, and Mr Dalur wanted to remain in contact with his daughter.

Hence the notes where a Corlesian code was written to name the time and place where they would meet. On the night Lija went missing, she received another note, just as she had in the past. But this was not written by Mr Dalur. Was it?"

Wolflock thrust the note found at the warehouses under Mr Dalur's nose, who shook his head and trembled.

"I... I never sent her a note that evening... that was the evening...We..."

His eyes fell on his wife and his face began to grow red.

"You've moving back to Corl, are you not?"

He paused for a long time before he mumbled, "Yes."

"You decided it two nights ago, correct?"

"Yes."

"And have you been receiving correspondence from Ms Vuori over the last two days?"

"She said she was happy to be rid of us. That she would perhaps send updates about Lija's life, but she would allow free and open correspondence to ease both of our suffering. That was what made me accept the decision in the end."

"I wrote to you once to tell you that Lija was

missing. I received your one letter back," Ms Vuori cried.

"That can't be... I have notes in your writing!" he patted himself down and then turned to his wife. "I gave them all to Ameiloe to send to you to ease her worries. I... she said it made her feel more confident in our marriage to read my mail and take the care to send it." He flung his hand out towards his wife, who stiffened and looked out of the window.

"And thus was the reason they never reached their destination," Wolflock sneered. "Now, Mrs Dalur," he placed both his hands on the arms of her chair and brought his nose inches from hers, "jealousy is a terrible thing to allow control over your heart and mind. Lying is just as bad."

She stayed as still as a statue, but her nose wrinkled with disgust.

"She has been burning your outgoing letters." Wolflock produced the letter he'd saved by the fire when they first sat in the parlour. "She is likely to have sent away your servants on completely unrelated business to maintain this façade. She has been forging the responses from Ms Vuori and, to top it all off, she was the one who forged the letter to Lija the night she went missing. We have all of her practice forgeries here."

The room was pin drop silent. Everyone stared at

Mrs Dalur.

"But... What proof do you have that I wrote any of those? You can't bring so-called evidence in my house and tell these people it was I," Mrs Dalur sniffed, staring down her nose at Wolflock.

"Your letters have the distinct scent of your perfume, as well as traces of the hand cream you use. A specific brand from Eastern Grothener if I'm not mistaken. Masters of creams and ointments." Wolflock opened the lid of the hand cream on the side table by Mrs Dalur's chair and indulged himself by massaging it into his own hands. "There is also the simple matter of the handwriting. It is so uncannily similar to yours, Mr Dalur, that it would have only been replicated by thorough and intense study. You may also note her complete and utter rage at writing the name of your daughter, as shown by the ferocity of which the pen was pressed into the paper. My only question is: Did you do it because you wanted to move on to this new Troston man? Who, I might add, seems to have dubious intentions as it is, let alone offering you no proof he will wed you once in Corl. Or did you do it because Mr Dalur loved his daughter more than he loved you?"

Tears started to stream down Mrs Dalur's cheeks, but she kept her back as stiff as a board, whispering something so quietly Wolflock had to ask, "What was that?"

"I just wanted to go back home. I just needed her away for one night. But, if anyone found out that I was the one who sent her that letter, then of course he'd choose to stay here."

"But... I thought you liked it in Mystentine. You always said you were happy as long as I was happy," Mr Dalur pleaded.

"I LIED!" She shrieked, standing up so abruptly that Wolflock had to jump back. "I LIED! I HATE IT HERE! I HATE THIS HOUSE! I HATE THIS CITY! I HATE YOUR MISTRESS AND I HATE YOUR SPAWN! THIS CITY IS FILLED WITH SIN! EVEN THIS PITIFUL CHURCH HAS NO BEAUTY! I HAVE NOTHING!"

"You have me," he protested weakly.

"YOU LEFT!" She fell to her knees in hysterics, sobbing into her hands. "You left for a woman who could give you a child, and I had to keep telling you it was fine. That I was fine. You broke my heart and my faith, and I still had to stay by your side. You even flaunted your spawn here in front of me. You gave her everything she asked for and I was left to collect dust with the furniture. I just wanted her away for one forsaken night so I could get you to take me back to Corl. Just one night and she still must rule over me! Oh he was right... he was so right..."

"Why not just tell Lija to stay home that night?" Mothy coaxed, holding Ms Vuori's arm so she didn't attack Mrs Dalur.

"That never worked. She's the only thing he ever put above all else. And, if she heard I wanted to have a private night with him, she'd come around just to spite me... she's done it before... he was right..."

"Who was right?" Wolflock asked and rested a hand on her shoulder as he knelt down too.

Mrs Dalur gasped. "No! I won't say his name. I won't let him get in trouble, too. He's the only true believer in this town, and he's been my only friend since I arrived. I won't throw him to the dogs. Trostons like us are persecuted and ridiculed throughout the land, and we have to stand together."

"Please, Mrs Dalur." Mothy knelt with them and hugged her. The room sat in shock, but none so much as Wolflock, who thought his friend had become mad. "You have a chance to do the right thing. We will make sure Mr Dalur takes you back to Corl, but you need to do the right thing now and help us make sure Lija is safe. That will make amends for your transgressions and Mr

Dalur will do everything he can to make amends for his."

She sniffled and hiccupped into Mothy's shoulder before melting into his tender arms and nodding.

"He...he..."

She dropped her shoulders and shook her head.

Wolflock and Mothy waited, but Captain Estivan stepped in. "Well, perhaps you'll care more about the life of a child at the station. Mrs Ameiloe Dalur, you are under arrest for the kidnapping and conspiracy to kidnap Mis Lija Vuori. Officer Tand, escort this woman back to the headquarters."

Officer Tand moved obediently, but Wolflock saw her biting her lip.

She's not convinced Mrs Dalur will break under his interrogation... And neither am I.

CHAPTER 8

Dangerous Child's Play

"Officer Estivan," Wolflock leaped forward, "wait! She didn't steal Lija-"

"But she knows who did. And that's 'Captain Estivan', boy."

Wolflock had one Captain, and it wasn't this man. He deferred by simply not addressing him by name. "She may know who did, but, without being delicate, she won't say a word."

"And you call what you just did delicate?"

"Surgical. She had no escape but to lie and she couldn't produce a lie I didn't have evidence to refute."

"Well, if what you do is called surgery, what we do is much the same. You have a lot of doubt for someone who has never seen the process before. Come along and watch. Maybe you'll learn a thing or two." Estivan clapped him on the shoulder and escorted Mrs Dalur out.

Mr Dalur looked to Ms Vuori as if asking permission to follow his wife. She ignored him, turning to Mothy and Wolflock.

"That... wasn't what was meant to happen, was it?"

"I don't think so," Mothy answered, but Wolflock had already left the room, heading straight for Theod.

The others followed him out and, without another word, jumped into the buggy, following Tand and Estivan back to the Guard Station. Theod pulled up at the Children's Protection Division building, but Estivan and Tand moved Mrs Dalur to another building. Wolflock realised that there was no interview room in their department. It was all open desks. He checked the door, but it was locked.

He jiggled it again and growled.

"We have to get," he tried once more, "a key. Gods dammit."

"Language," Mothy scolded, kneeling to look at the lock. "They didn't leave the key in the lock, but, if you pass me your pen knife, I might be able to get it open."

Wolflock patted himself down and shook his head. "It must be in my trunk."

"Uh... what about a hairpin?"

"Do I look like I use hairpins?"

Ms Vuori drew out a slender hatpin out of her black hat from amongst the lacey frills.

"You should be using hairpins." Mothy mumbled as he slid the thin metal between the latch and panel.

"What's that supposed to mean?" Wolflock asked as he leaned casually against the wall.

"All I'm saying is that your hair is getting long enough that you've had to blow it out of your face. Could be a hazard, is all."

"You're a hazard," Wolflock laughed through his nose.

"Not to this door, I'm not. Sorry, Ms Vuori. Hatpins are a bit too round for this." He turned around and passed the pin back to the Antrum woman.

Wolflock looked up and his blood froze.

Officer Tand glared up at them. "A key works better."

She walked up the five stairs and shoved her key in the lock, walking as if the others weren't even there.

"Well, do you want to get kidnapped too?" She heaved a sigh as she made her way to her desk, flopping into her seat behind the mountain of files on her desk.

"Sorry?" Wolflock asked, peeking between the stacks of manilla leaking with poorly filed reports.

"Apparently, I'm the reason the children have gone missing recently, including Lija."

"I still don't follow."

Officer Tand looked up at Ms Vuori with her hazel eyes filled with concern. "My insubordination. I'm the one who let Lija see the captain's basement and that broke down the chain of command, rules, regulations, and the very fabric of our society."

Ms Vuori sighed. "She would have found a way in. She's the most determined child I know. With unhealthy levels of curiosity." She teared up again and Officer Tand passed her a handkerchief. "What did she want in there anyway?"

"She wouldn't say. She said it was essential for her to know but I just thought she was being nosy since Captain Estivan told her off for trying to get down there the other day. Do you think Mrs Dalur conspired to kidnap Lija with the dark-haired man?"

The officer put her forehead on her fingertips. "No. The Captain is too excited to finally have someone in custody for all this. He's not thinking clearly. With all the stress we're under, he's desperate for a win. This isn't right, though."

"You don't think having Mrs Dalur in custody will give us more time to find Lija?" Wolflock asked as he began going through Captain Estivan's desk, making sure he slanted everything just a little. Many of the case files before him seemed out of place and petty. Some had nothing to do with children and others looked like they belonged with a less serious department. His mind flicked them together with the merest cursory glances.

Mrs Griknan's pocket watch was sold by her resentful daughter. Mr Plumper is lying about the stolen book on magical circles so he can steal ideas from his competition. The dog doesn't belong to either Mr Yimms or Mr Felu, so just ask where it wants to live. The missing grandmother left with her woodcutter partner and is likely to be found on a beach in Shellinmerth, avoiding her irritating family.

"No. I think it might alert the kidnapper that we're on to them. What if they do something-" she froze and looked at Ms Vuori, who stared tearfully back at the blue clad officer.

Wolflock didn't like the growing tension and despondency. "So, walk me through the evening you showed Lija how to get into Estivan's secret room."

Officer Tand glared up at him through the files

before she rolled her eyes and shoved her chair out. "Check behind the panel of his name stand."

Wolflock tilted his head, impressed, as he drew out a small flat key. "Have you been in there?"

"No. Not since the captain locked it up."

Wolflock put the key in the lock under the forbidden door's handle with a smirk. "Do you want to?"

The other three in the room rushed over and, when the door opened, raced onto a set of stairs that lead down and back around under the office.

Wolflock lit his bone match and saw two long tables and a six-foot-long cork board with brass pins holding pictures of fifteen children's sketched faces and some string connecting them to various letters and documents.

"Are these... Are they all...?" Ms Vuori breathed.

Wolflock felt a chill he wouldn't admit to. All his lightness about the situation and the fun he'd felt about solving the puzzle dissolved as the reality of the situation set in.

Olgeir, 10, Found shoe at scene, dragged, no struggle. Last seen 61 Unglegt Passage.

Bodvar, 8, Found doll brother made, no struggle. Last seen park on Penna Street

Freybjorn, 9, Lamp lighter reported man talking to

them before carried away. Last seen park on Brunn Avenue.

Blarn 7, Too dark to see but reports of talking to older person. Last seen 595 Warehouses and Storage

Saebur, 9, No description could be given. Last seen at children's shelter and said new job was here. Last seen 595 Warehouses and Storage

Sandri, 11, Refused company and said working, no sign of struggle.

Asbjornson, 10, No sign of struggle. Last seen Schmeid Community Blacksmiths

Bryn, 9, walked off with thin man, said working good job, too dark. No description. Last seen Silfur Square

Finnbo, 12, Leaving station after picked up for petty theft. Vanished before left border. Last seen Silfur Square asking for younger brother Brynn.

Elbert, 6, Library assistant position helping other children read. Last seen waiting for librarian to lock up and walk her to temple.

Falka, 10, artist redecorating warehouses. Last seen 595 Warehouses and Storage

Halmpor, 7, Butcher apprentice. Last seen leaving temple after bathing. Sleeps there.

Marsson, 10, Questioned in relation to brawl by Silfur Square Fountain. Last seen leaving Guard Station.

Aolfson, 9, Questioned in relation to petty theft. Last seen leaving Guard Station.

Each child's sketched portrait had a pin, from which a blue string tacked from their picture over the large map showing where they normally loitered. A red string led to where they were last seen. A wormwood green string streaked away to smaller names on the map for relevant witnesses.

The dates on the disappearances stretched back six weeks.

Other pins scattered around the board had details about suspected gambling dens, illegal substance manufacturers, illegal brewers, and citizens who had displayed uncharacteristic behaviour.

Wolflock's throat clenched as he read, then looked at the children's faces. None of them were older than twelve. No parents, living in shelters or temples. He could barely comprehend what had gotten them there or what prospects they'd have as they grew up, but to vanish away like this was terrifying.

The door banged upstairs and everyone but Wolflock jumped. He narrowed his eyes at the board, as if daring it to try and withhold its patterns. He expected Captain Estivan to return and find the basement door open.

He expected him to come downstairs and begin rousing on them. He expected to have a few stern words with the man.

But the banging door was proceeded by silence. The person had clearly seen the forbidden door open. Perhaps it was Chestir, and his brain had short circuited that someone else had messed up the disorganisation of the office worse than him.

Quick footsteps creaked the floorboards above them into the mid back of the office.

Isn't that near Chestir's desk? Wolflock allowed a single train of attention to follow them as he saw a pattern forming on the map.

"They're all away from main roads, avoiding purely residential districts, avoiding wealthy areas, and... I'm missing something. Tand, what do you see in this?" Wolflock muttered, hoping the officer had better insight into the city than he did.

She refixed her officer's cap and scanned them with the ferocious focus of a hunter. "Let's say the captain thought these were connected, each one would have been manageable on its own, but, between the gambling dens and other crimes being stretched across the city, the Guards weren't able to attend to the cases with less evidence."

"That's it." Wolflock clapped his hands once. "On the same day the gambling dens and manufacturers were raided, on the other side of the district some kind of disturbance happened that was large enough to draw the weight of the Guard. Then, always along the same roads between the Guard Station and Silfur Square, a child goes missing."

The wood creaked above them and the door slammed shut again. Glad to not be interrupted, Wolflock continued.

"You're missing the warehouses. They're nowhere near the roads you're talking about."

He pinched his chin in thought, looking over the map for more clues. Then he saw a familiar symbol pinned with a black pin on the side. The 't' shape with the eye arching over the top three stems. Exactly the same one Mothy had burnt into his back. A note written beneath it was that Lija told the children to avoid it. Black pins only sat in two locations, and one was barely a block away from the warehouses.

"Why is there a Troston church in the manufacturing district?" he asked Officer Tand. "Why is it not near the other temples?"

Tand pulled a face. "They upset the other temples and people attending. When they aren't proselytising, they're ranting about how the end of days is nigh and everyone is living in sin. By law they're allowed to practise their religion as they see fit, as long as it harms none, and keeping them away from the other temples means they don't hurt anyone else."

Mothy stood beside Wolflock with worry etching across his soft features. He'd seen what Wolflock had.

"Surely not... not in Mystentine. This is the city built on freedom and escaping that!" He shook, unable to pry the words from his throat. "Lockie... not with children."

Wolflock wanted to dismiss it as speculation, or a poor representation of another symbol, but the history and the images were too alike.

"This isn't just about Lija, anymore. Trostons are known for promoting slavery. This looks like a coordinated development of illegal industries in a city that hasn't had to deal with them on this scale before. He's running rings around the local constabulary by using a religious structure as a front for this. There's evidence of mind controlling powders, kidnapping, illegal gambling, and an increase in substance dependency."

"If he's been so prolific, why haven't we been able to catch hide nor hair of him?" Officer Tand snapped, flinging her hand out and knocking over a stack of files beside the board.

Then it struck him.

"Because..." he knelt down and picked up one of

Lija's drawings that had flown from the pile, "he's part of the Guard. And Lija knew it."

He held up the picture she'd drawn of a man in blue with dark, short hair and a nasty face crumpling papers of missing persons pictures.

"If she knew who it was, why didn't she tell anyone? Why did she talk to them at the warehouses?" Ms Vuori cried, clutching the picture to her chest.

Heavy slow footsteps turned down the stairs and Captain Estivan appeared with his face pinched. Wolflock couldn't see anger, but, rather, regret.

"She did tell someone. She was working for me."

"Captain! I-I'm so sorry. We just-I-" Officer Tand stammered.

"At ease, Tand. I couldn't keep this a secret any longer, and I trust you more than anyone else on the Guard."

"Captain." She nodded, respectfully.

"What have you done?" Ms Vuori's lip trembled. "What did you do to my daughter?"

Captain Estivan's shoulders slumped. "Lija is the brightest, most determined child I know. She reported all of these children missing before anyone else. She had her finger on the pulse better than us. She snuck down here and found my board a week before she went missing. At first, I was mad at her for overstepping, but then she fought back because she believed I was lying to the street children. I made her a deal. I would let her help me if she... if she could find the person I suspected was destroying evidence."

Officer Tand smacked her forehead. "That's why she was following me. She thought it was me. That's why she wanted to come down here again."

"Where did she follow you to?"

Officer Tand pointed to the end of the line of disappearances. "Silfur Square."

"That's where you've been meeting," Wolflock paused, "friends."

Officer Tand flushed crimson and coughed. "Yes. I thought that meeting there in my downtime would deter any crime. I have to collect files from Chestir's apartment near there too, sometimes, if he's accidentally taken them home."

"Does that happen often?" Wolflock asked.

"I mean, more often lately. If you haven't noticed, Chestir's been clumsier and more scattered than usual."

"What are you talking about, Tand? He's been picking up the slack that other clerks have been letting slip?" Captain Estivan frowned.

"Umm, with all due respect, sir, Chestir is useless. He mixes up files, loses evidence, mis-records statements, and then blames everyone else for it. He used to be effective, but he has been slipping for months." Officer Tand lifted her chin.

A silence fell between the authorities, the only noise came from Ms Vuori crinkling the drawing in her hands.

"Why isn't Eric Thomezsi on your board? I can't see an Eric Thomezsi." Wolflock looked at her hands and took out the piece of crumpled paper. She had been holding a list of twenty names along the sketch of a dark haired man. It looked like one of Lija's drawings. The first ten names were crossed out. The eleventh was Eric Thomezsi.

"Lija was looking for the face by eliminating names," Wolflock muttered to himself.

"There's no report of a missing Eric." Captain Estivan frowned.

"That's because he's not missing." Wolflock ripped out the small painting he'd taken from Mrs Dalur's case and held it up for Ms Vuori. "Is this the man you gave your statement to?" She quivered her head in a little nod. "He's the culprit. He's the dark-haired man. He stood right there, in the office upstairs, and took Ms Vuori's statement the morning she found her daughter was missing."

Ms Vuori let out a small scream. Officer Tand and Mothy ran to her side in support.

"He was in Silfur Square the night Lija saw you and

your friend, the night she went missing. He... he was there last night again, smoking." Wolflock paced back and forth around the room. "Or, at least, his friend was"

"Smoking?" Officer Tand spoke up.

The pungent scent of tobacco in Wolflock's memory triggered a thought. He'd seen someone else smoke. "Chestir knows who the dark-haired man is."

Without another word he raced from the room, hurtled up the stairs and swung around a mountain of files to Chestir's desk.

An ashtray sat on the desk, mounded with cigarette butts. Wolflock opened the files on his desk, flicking through them for anything relevant, then threw them on the floor. It wasn't like the files were well put together anyway. Wrong names, irrelevant evidence, illegible witness statements, and caricatures of Officer Tand and Captain Estivan. Not finding what he wanted in the files, he upturned the bin and started unrolling the crumpled papers.

"Lockie, what's your thinking?" Mothy asked, leading the line of people out of the basement.

"Help me find Ms Vuori's report. He probably took it and threw it out."

Mothy took over the paper bin and Wolflock yanked open the feeble draws. They were locked, but the key left in one of the locks fit all of them. Wolflock jumped back as something furry rolled forward in the draw.

"What is it?" Mothy looked up at his shocked friend.

"A wig."

A chestnut wig.

"It's horsehair. That's why it looked off."

Under the wig was a pair of thick glasses.

"Hey, Lockie. I didn't just find the report. Look. All these pieces of evidence are stamped from different departments. Why are they in the trash?"

Wolflock found an old receipt tucked up the back of Chestir's middle drawer for the 595 Warehouses.

"Mothy, look."

595 Fjallafoss Warehouses and Storage
Date: Eolas Revari, Culimpus, 4th. Rayin 7th Year
Single warehouse lease, three years
Price: 52 Deimas
Customer Signature: Astraxis Smjunt

"Why would Chestir have a receipt signed by Astraxis?" Mothy frowned.

Wolflock looked around the room at Ms Vuori, Officer Tand and Captain Estivan. His eyes fell on his poorly labelled name stand.

Chestir Moi'ez.

Wolflock ripped the paper out of the stand and scribbled down the name, rearranging the letters.

"Because he's been orchestrating the launch of a new criminal enterprise in Mystentine for Astraxis. That's why all of this has been so organised. He's been collecting children to sell for when Astraxis arrives in the city any day now. And his name isn't Chestir Moi'ez. It's Eric Thomezsi."

No one could argue that the evidence of the wig and anagram made sense.

"But where is Lija?" Ms Vuori trembled with fear and grief.

Wolflock shook the warehouse rental receipt. "She's been under our noses the entire time."

Rhiannon D. Elton

CHAPTER 9

The Final Move

aptain Estivan," Wolflock barked. "Gather as many of the Guard as you can. This will be the end to most of their dilemmas, so I expect them to be pulled from their regular duties. I need you to surround the warehouses owned by Saraesh and Mr Dalur. Only this group is to go in or out and none of them are to know what is going on. We don't know who else has been helping Chestir."

"You think this is where Lija is being held?" Captain Estivan asked.

"I think that's where all the children are being held.

169

There may also be dangerous or illegal products there. We need to act with the utmost caution. Get Mr Dalur and a carriage, and meet us there. We'll discuss our plan of attack in the office after it's locked down. Mothy, Ms Vuori, come with me."

He raced from the room and shouted for Theod to move with the greatest speed.

"Fear not, Mr Felen, my hooves are blessed with lightning and my flanks with wind!"

Had the situation not been so dire, the boys would have snickered, but their faces were held like stone as they raced through the city streets in the late afternoon light. The sense that the web of clues had been solved didn't overshadow the feeling of a looming spider racing them to the centre.

"Theod, we may need you for a particularly important mission. How do you feel about apprehending a villain?" Wolflock shouted over the wind of their galloping drive.

"What a thrill!" the horse whinnied.

"That's what I like to hear! I need you to patrol the streets surrounding the warehouses and, if anyone comes out with children, you need to stop them. Understand?"

"Save the little ones. Got it."

Wolflock tried to think of other ways he could

block off their departure from the warehouses, but his gut churned at the thought that they may already be too late.

Soon, Theod came to a rapid halt in front of the warehouses. He leaped down and bashed through the door, seeing Saraesh jump up in alarm.

"It's you! What's the matter?"

"Has anyone left here today?" he slammed his hands on the counter, his blue eyes as wide as saucers.

"N-no! Why? What's wrong?"

"Saraesh, we need a map, and we need you to make sure all the gates are locked. No one is to go in or out of the storage facility. Lija is here."

"P-pardon?"

Ms Vuori gripped the bench with even whiter knuckles. "My. Daughter. Is. Here. Don't waste time with stupid questions! Do what he says!"

"Y-yes, ma'am! I'm sorry. Map. Yes. Schematics. Blueprints. Everything you need." The large, tanned woman ran to the office room and broke a frame from the wall, bringing out a map of the warehouses. Over the glass with thick watercolour paints was marked what was in them. She slammed it onto the counter. "Anything else?"

Ms Vuori's eyes welled with tears as she looked down. "Tissues. Got it. I'll get those too."

"The block is a perfect rectangle with a large gate at the back, a large one at the front, and a doorway exit beside each of them. There are no ways out to the sides. What about sewerage?"

"The office here has a bathroom and there is a maintenance hole to the sewers by the back gate. The channels lead onto the streets for water drainage." Saraesh jogged back in, giving the quilted box of tissues to Ms Vuori.

"Excellent. Can anyone come in to collect or view their storage at any time?"

"They have to come through the office and check in. It's how I prevent theft. They have a key to their shed, but we always have one attendant and one guard on the premises."

"And where is the guard now?"

Saraesh bit her lip. "I was still waiting for him to arrive. He's late for his shift. We only had three people come in for their storage this afternoon."

"What?" Wolflock shouted. "Who?"

"I-it was, uh..." she snatched up the clipboard from the wall behind her and ran her finger down to the last three entries. "Mr Fjorn Manteil, warehouse four. Mr Natien Thork, warehouse five, and Astraxis Smjunt in warehouse eleven."

"Well that's it then, isn't it? Warehouse eleven?" Mothy asked, poking the map at warehouse eleven.

Wolflock frowned. "No. Each of these warehouses are as far away from one another as they can be. Did these three men come in together?"

"Yes. Only a quarter of an hour before you arrived. Astraxis said he was awaiting a transport carriage and that he'd be taking some of his belongings this evening."

For a moment Wolflock's gut flipped. Was it the real Astraxis? Or Chestir, Eric impersonating him?

"What did he look like?"

"Tall, slim, uh... not the best dressed, but not unclean."

"His hair?"

"I don't know. He wore a bowler hat."

Mothy grabbed Wolflock's arm. "What are you thinking?"

He pinched the bridge of his nose and crammed his eyes shut. "They know they're discovered. Chestir has been given ample time to tip them off. They'll be desperate to escape. We want to get the children to safety. Apprehending them is secondary to the children's safety. Watch out for any kinds of drinking alcohol as it may be flammable. We must act now. Saraesh, go and lock everything as quickly as you can. Ms Vuori, follow her around and then go to number eleven. It's under Astraxis' name, so it's likely to be the one we're after. Check every box, knock on every surface, and know that the children may be under the effects of the Lady Mind Master, so if they aren't themselves, don't worry. A good splash of water and wild lettuce will fix that right up. Mothy, you go to number four and, if anything goes wrong, run back to the office and lock the door. I know you're fast enough to do it."

Mothy nodded, setting his shoulders with determination.

"I'll take number five."

Saraesh locked the front gate and door exit, then gave an office key to Mothy. Her and Ms Vuori set out towards the back of the facility together. Mothy gripped Wolflock's sleeve with his crystal blue eyes glinting with concern.

"You are the stupidest smart person I know, Lockie. Don't you dare get hurt. Not for anything dumb, aye? We have a mountain to climb together."

"Same to you."

The pair hugged tightly for a moment, then set off in opposite directions. Wolflock's shoes tapped against the cobblestone pathways, splashing the slips of water sitting in the grooves of the stones. The dusty orange sunset cast long dark shadows between the sheds. The fifth shed's lock was open, and the chain draped through the large hole in the door.

He peeked in but couldn't see anything in the darkness. He heard the other doors being opened, and listened for any calls, but the rolling metal wheels fell quiet. Wolflock used all his strength to shift the door, groaning as he got it open enough for two people to fit through. He lit his bone match and looked around. Huge crates sat stacked in three rows leading all the way down to the back of the shed. Without hesitation he looked for gaps to peek in, and when he couldn't find any, he jammed his penknife between the boards and created a gap. When the lids were within his reach, he opened them.

Fabric. Linen. Candles in straw. Tapestries. Incense. All things to fit out a temple. He hadn't expected Chestir or Astraxis to be using the storage for legitimate business as well as nefarious ones. He still hadn't heard anything from the other sheds, though.

Scowling, Wolflock exited the shed and saw the lights start to come on between the buildings. He looked over at the sixth shed, where Lija had last been seen. Something looked strange about the chain. Someone had tucked it into the hole, so it looked like it was locked from the inside. Wolflock walked over to it and pulled the chain out. It was unlocked.

Saraesh had mentioned yesterday that they had a strange set of break-ins and an administrator who left abruptly. What if he had changed the lock on this shed so he didn't leave evidence of renting it? Saraesh had said he had short, dark hair.

Wolflock's eyes went wide, and he shoved the door. It had been opened far more frequently than number five and rolled with oiled wheels.

It's almost silent, Wolflock thought as he slipped inside. He couldn't hear a sound. No breathing, no shuffling. No chatter. He raised the match, casting a light around the warehouse. No movement, but similar large crates were stacked in the same formation. As he moved through them, tapping on them with his knuckles, he saw the centre boxes were bolted to one another. They also sounded hollow. He tried to shove his pen knife into the planks to see inside them, but it hit a harder surface. Someone had lined them with metal or stone.

His match light glinted on something shiny above him.

He looked up and saw a shiny hinge bulging out of the top of the stack. Without hesitation, he climbed up. Before him sat a six-foot-tall box with one side that looked more like a door. A large iron barrel latch was all that was locking it. He turned the heavy latch and lifted it to the side, wedging it open before he pulled the door as far open as it would go.

The first thing that struck him was the terrible smell that poured out of the strange shell of boxes. Sweat, blood, hopelessness and organic waste poured out, and it smelled worse than anything that had ever touched his nostrils before. He stepped into the boxes with his hand raising the match ahead of him and his left hand covering his mouth and nose with his handkerchief.

Then, he turned the corner into a cramped metal room with thirteen filthy children huddled together.

"He's alone! Get him!" one shouted and ran at Wolflock with savage claws.

He raised his arm just in time to save his face as she slashed at him.

"Wait! Wait! I'm here to release you!" he shouted as she sliced through his shirt.

"It's not him, Lija!" piped up one of the smallest girls, dashing forward to grab the taller, pale girl.

Her flaming red eyes were unmistakable.

"Lija Vuori?" Wolflock grimaced in pain as he clutched his arm.

"How do you know my name?"

"Your mother sent me. I'm here to get you home."

Lija looked like she wanted to believe Wolflock, but she stayed back, keeping her hands taunt and ready to attack.

"Prove it! Prove my mother sent you."

Wolflock stammered for a moment. "Uh... You sent secret messages to your father in his home language?"

"I don't believe you! Mama wouldn't know that! They said to Yeesa they'd take her home if she was good and she only got beat!" she yelled and threw her arms out to protect the younger children. "I can't even believe Captain Estivan! Not after..."

"Not after what?"

"He told me I had an important mission. I was meant to find the bad guy and I followed the evidence here. Then, it wasn't who I thought it was and I fell asleep after talking to- Oh no! I shouldn't have said anything! I promised I wouldn't!" She gasped and covered her mouth with her free hand.

"It's all fine, Lija. I know about Captain Estivan's mission for you. I saw the board he made looking for all the children. That's how I found you. With the help of all your clues."

"I was meant to help," she sniffed as her eyes

welled up with angry tears. "And now I'm trapped in this stupid cave in the middle of nowhere!

Wolflock dropped to one knee so he could see most of the children in the eye, smiling through the pain searing through his arm.

"Lija, we are in one of the warehouses your father owns. We just need to go outside, and you'll see your parents. I'll help you all get out. How does that sound? I promise I won't hurt any of you. I don't have any weapons and I don't stand a chance against all of you. But, we have to get out of here in case the people that brought you all here come back."

At his final sentence Lija nodded and waved for the rest to get up, keeping a close eye on him and the door.

"Help us out. You come out last," she said sternly, pointing a thick sharp nail at Wolflock's chest. He chuckled and admired her courage with a nod.

He helped lift all the children up the ledge to the exit and watched as they scrambled out.

"It is the warehouse, Lija!" one of the children cried out as he lifted Lija onto the sloping box floor and heaved himself out after. To delay anyone knowing the children had escaped their imprisonment, Wolflock relatched the entrance crate.

"You..." she breathed as Wolflock hopped down beside her, "you really did come to save us!"

He was winded when she threw her arms around his middle and hugged him, but he shushed her and got the children to follow him behind the centre boxes.

"Everyone here?" he looked back and smiled, still counting thirteen children.

A light moving into the shed caught his eye and he doused his match. At first, he thought it was Saraesh, but the person coming in was far too thin to be her. The figure stepped inside with two others dressed in Guard uniforms.

"Stay quiet," Wolflock mouthed to Lija, who put her finger to her lips and gestured for all the children around her to do the same.

Wolflock leaned back and peeked over the boxes, seeing the exit guarded by the thin man.

"When the other idiots get here, look busy and keep them away. I'll douse the stock again and make sure they're quiet."

"Yes boss," the burly pair answered in unison.

Wolflock glared, but, as his heart pounded, he had a flash of inspiration.

"Lija," he whispered, "Your mother and Saraesh are looking for you. You're in warehouse six. Do you know where eleven is?"

She nodded.

"Good. I'm going to distract these buffoons. I need you to help the other children go around the other side of these boxes and sneak out. Then, when you're out, run for warehouse eleven. Officer Tand and Estivan will be here soon. Tell your mother and Saraesh to get everyone into the office and lock the doors if they can. Understand."

She nodded again but bit her bottom lip with worry. "But what's going to happen to you?"

Wolflock forced a smile. "Don't you worry about me. I've handled bigger and uglier fiends than him. We just have to wait for a moment."

Chestir tapped his foot, scratched his head, and growled in frustration. "Where the devil is our transport?"

"Everything good, boss?" one of the burly dullards asked.

"No. Everything is not good. Go and check on the cargo. Do something useful," he snapped as he yanked on another chestnut wig and lit a cigarette.

The two men shuffled their feet towards the crates and rolled onto the boxes. Wolflock was thankful that Chestir hogged the lantern, keeping the back of the warehouse shrouded in shadow. The dark haired boy pressed his hands on the crate in front of him and swung his legs up. Taking a breath and holding it, Wolflock pressed his back to the back of the crate, just out of view.

The first ruffian opened the door and swung it so hard Wolflock had to grip his nose to stop from shouting in pain.

"Hey, you gotta light? I can't see nuffin'."

"You're just blind," responded the second.

Wolflock waved to Lija to get ready, and, the moment both men had stepped inside the crate, he threw all his weight against the door and shoved the latch down.

"Chestir!" he cried out triumphantly. "Chestir! Come quickly! I've got the kidnappers!"

The burly men banged against the door and Wolflock heard one fall backwards with a satisfying 'dong' noise.

"What?" Chestir snapped, then lifted his light to see Wolflock pretending to hold the door closed.

"I need help! Quickly! The door won't hold."

To Wolflock's immense satisfaction, Chestir's face writhed with fury as he charged forward. Lija and the others made their way to the door out, just out of view.

"Thank goodness you've found them." Chester's nasally voice sounded saccharine. "I'm sure they're secure, let me look at the latch here. We need to take them in for questioning."

"Haha. Nice try, Chestir. Nice try." Wolflock snickered. "You can't have all the glory for yourself, now. You'll have to go halves in it, at least."

"You've just locked the kidnappers in there with the children. That's not very safe, is it?" The fake clerk's eyes darted around for a way to get Wolflock away. "Sergeant Estivan has sent us down to help collect the little ones and return them to their families after he received Tand's note. You've made Mystentine a safer place this evening. I wouldn't take that away from you."

"Ah, yes. Of course. Tand's note. The one referring to all the evidence we have right here. The evidence indicating the kidnapper has been part of the Guard itself all along."

"Yes, yes, yes. All of which you shall be handing over immediately to be processed."

"Yes, certainly. Let me just clarify, though. Tand sent Captain Estivan a note saying which warehouse we would be in and the specific evidence we had against this villain? Like the wig and receipt for the storage shed?"

"Do not test me, boy. Hand over what you have now!" Chester snapped savagely and stepped back from the door, keeping his hand on the latch.

"The funny thing is, I specifically told Tand and Captain Estivan to not disclose any information about this evening and keep everyone around the perimeter."

"Well, she doesn't answer to you, does she?"

"We also didn't find the warehouse until we got here."

"She saw you come in here."

"Oh really?" Wolflock smirked and puffed out his chest. "And what evidence was described in her note?"

"Enough of this!" Chester shrieked and launched himself at Wolflock, who held out his elbow firmly and collected the man in the face, knocking him dazedly off the crates.

Wolflock rubbed his elbow and hopped down off the crates with a grin. With a confident swagger, he intended on locking Chestir and his cronies in the shed until Tand and Estivan got there to put them in custody. As he reached the door, he heard Chestir get to his feet and cough.

"Wait," he groaned.

Wolflock smirked and leaned against the door, watching the de-wigged man limp towards him.

"You know, I didn't like you to begin with, but weaponised incompetence is a whole new trick. You made the captain believe you were fixing everyone else's mistakes, while doing a terrible job in order to cover for your own. I don't think my pride would ever let me do that." Wolflock picked at his nails.

"You found out everything, didn't you?" the dark-haired man winced, hobbling closer.

"Oh yes, Eric. Everything. I guess you thought you were clever using an anagram of your own name as your alias, Chestir Moi'ez, Eric Thomezsi. It made you easier to discover in the end. You know, Lija figured it out first though. She gave us your name, all the children that were missing, everything. I can only take the credit for following her cryptic breadcrumbs. There is one thing I hadn't quite figured out that you could help me with," Wolflock added, preparing himself to slam the door closed and latch the chain.

"Oh?"

"How did you subdue the children? I didn't find any purple powder anywhere. You didn't feed it to them, did you? You're not meant to do that. Astraxis's orders."

Eric's face twitched as he tried to maintain his composure. "Oh no," he breathed, holding his ribs. "I don't need that. I have something that is my own blend of sleep powder."

"Sleep powder? I'm not sure if that's better or worse than the whole mind control thing." Wolflock rolled his eyes, checking the lane outside for any movement as he waved his hand.

Clouds washed over the sky, and it darkened in the shed, but Wolflock's vision didn't brighten. He felt his head move as if he were in slow motion, and too late did he realise he'd let Eric get too close. He hadn't been holding his ribs, he'd been drawing out a bag of brown powder that he threw at Wolflock's face. His eyes stung and it whooshed up his nose as he coughed.

He tried to pull the door closed but his legs sank beneath him. He raised his arms but felt something impact his gut. Eric's hand launched himself at him and he saw a flurry of fists flashing in front of a face filled with pure hatred.

Wolflock felt a crack behind his head, followed by a hot wetness, then a fist met his cheek, and a mass of blond hair and tan pants ripped the weight off him before everything went black. He had a foggy recollection of being lifted into weightlessness, then nothing but the beating of his own heart in his head.

CHAPTER 10

From Amateur to Adept

His face ached.

He was clean but his head felt like a balloon.

Wolflock tried to open his eyes, but he could barely see. On top of the balloon feeling was a cold, wet feeling. The room smelled like medicines, and he wondered if he was in the apothecary. He could tell that the swaying sensation came from his head, rather than the room moving like it would on the ship. He sat up slowly and felt his whole top half complain. His legs seemed fine, but his arm was sore, and his shoulders, neck and head felt like they'd been trampled by a horse.

"Oh! Lockie! You're awake. Fantastic!" Mothy's excited voice boomed next to him. As Wolflock peeled his eye open, he saw his friend had been sitting beside him, reading a booklet about Mystentine University.

"Moffy?" Wolflock slurred numbly, "Moffy, what happened?"

"Don't speak too much or you'll dribble. Doctor Växtadlare gave you some pain relief tonics and poultices that they made you talk in your sleep."

Wolflock stopped for a moment as he felt his head throb.

"What did I say?"

"I wrote most of it down." Mothy smiled and pulled out Wolflock's blue journal from the bag beside him. "You grumbled a lot about 'stupid' people. Seems like listing everyone in your hometown and calling them 'stupid' made you laugh. Thorn brothers... stupid. Fenck children... stupid. Gruss boys... stupid. Then you came a bit closer to the present chanting 'Captain of the Silver Bald Patch' over and over. After that you called out my name a few times as if you wanted to show me something, followed by a very cheeky 'nope'. I still want to know what that was. You also cried for your mum because the bad men had hit you-"

Wolflock swallowed and felt his cheeks get hot. He raised his hands, touching his face to see what the damage was.

Mothy took the hint and closed the journal, passing Wolflock a mirror. His face was a mottled black, purple, and crimson. Both his eyes were so swollen he could barely see, and his cut lip stung as soon as he saw it. A thick layer of green mush covered various areas and over his bare shoulders.

"All in the name of a noble cause, though right?" Mothy chuckled.

"If you say so..." Wolflock grumbled, unconvinced.

"I did tell you to not get hurt without a good reason, you dolt!" Mothy punched his arm and passed him a glass of white translucent liquid with a cobalt glass straw.

"What's this?"

"Doctor's orders. Drink up. It'll keep reducing the swelling."

"What is it, though?"

"Dunno. White stuff?" Mothy shrugged.

Wolflock drank the bitter tasting concoction and found that everything felt better.

"That's good stuff!" he remarked, smacking his lips, feeling like he could open his eyes even more.

"Good to know! Did you want me to get Captain Estivan now? Are you up for a chat?"

"Huh?"

"Well they're all downstairs waiting for you. I managed to get a rest, but they've hardly slept."

"Who are they?"

"Captain Estivan, Ms Vuori, Mr Dalur, Lija, Officer Tand, even Dr Växtadlare. All of them."

"What do they want?" Wolflock tried to frown but it made his face hurt.

"They want to know how you knew. All of it. They have so many questions I can't answer."

"Did you try?" Wolflock tried to raise his eyebrow. That hurt, too.

"Pfft! Nope. Didn't even hazard a guess. I think it adds to your air of mystique and intrigue."

Wolflock chuckled a little and winced. That hurt as well.

"Maybe send the doctor up with more white pain medicine and then I'll see them."

"I'll let them know."

While Mothy was gone, Wolflock had the distinct feeling of being watched. Glancing about the room he caught a glimpse of a little, purplish white hand and a bright red eye peeking around the doorframe.

Before he could say anything, Lija squeaked and ran away down the hall.

It took another hour after Doctor Växtadlare tended to his face for the swelling to go down enough for Wolflock to feel comfortable talking, but, eventually, Mothy helped him downstairs and he sat on one of the dark oak sofas. Everyone seemed to be holding their breath, waiting for Wolflock to speak. He rather enjoyed the suspense and took a long sip of tea, glanced around, and smiled at their bated attention.

He placed the ceramic cup down, took a breath, and then another sip of tea. It was quite good tea, with a hint of foreign spices and warmth.

Still no one spoke.

He went for a third sip but Mothy kicked his leg with a grin.

"Well," he coughed to clear his throat, "it is good to see you all. I presume you have questions."

Captain Estivan nodded and straightened his uniform. "Firstly, I wanted to let you know that we apprehended the two lackeys and Chestir. I mean, Eric. When Mothy attacked Eric, he managed to get the key and fled through the door, but your hansom horse caught him leaving and throttled him."

Wolflock chuckled, thinking Theod would love to add 'apprehender of villains' to his list of titles.

"The city is posting extra measures to ensure all of the things they had their fingers in are cleaned up. What I want to know is, how did you know Chestir was responsible for all of this?"

"Oh, he wasn't." Wolflock shook his head. "It was also Ms Vuori, Mr Dalur, Mrs Dalur, Officer Tand, and yourself who were responsible for Lija's abduction."

The room bustled angrily for a moment, but Wolflock raised his hand to settle them.

"Let me explain how and why. Lija has been under your mentorship for some time now, no?"

The Sergeant shifted uncomfortably.

"Around the same time, Lija was prohibited from seeing her father due to being struck by Mrs Dalur. She felt forced to see her father in secret, which appealed to her already adventurous nature. But going between the warehouses, where her father worked, and the Child Protection Division, particularly on the case which was relevant to the location of the warehouses, made her a potential threat to Chestir's operation. After hearing that she had been given access to your private sanctum that he couldn't tamper with, he made the opportunity to make sure Lija was out of the picture.

"It was all set up quite perfectly, yet entirely by coincidence. Mrs Dalur was pressured by her dark-haired suitor, Eric, to go back to Corl with all the evidence that would link him to the Troston church, his primary source of money, and his connection to the upper echelon he was selling slaves to, as well as gambling with. He told her that she needed an evening to discuss going back to Corl without Lija's interference, so she wrote a letter mimicking Mr Dalur's writing telling Lija to stay away for the evening. This would certainly keep the child away and also damage their relationship as Lija would have been quite hurt by this transgression. Being quite lonely in Mystentine, Mrs Dalur clung to the only other Troston she knew of here; Chestir, or Eric, being one that showed her a great deal of interest. Instead of keeping Lija away for the evening, Mrs Dalur was prompted by Chestir to send her to the warehouse. In her mind, the child would be more upset and more inclined to accept her father's move had he mistreated her.

"When Lija chatted with who she thought was Chestir on the night of her abduction, he coated her favourite lollies in a sleep powder and waited for them to take effect. Clearly, she trusted Chestir enough to eat those lollies without question. She'd been working with him and the Child Protection Division for months. He just had to encourage her to eat those lollies and wait for her to fall asleep. We saw the same effect on Mothy and Ms Vuori when we stayed the night at Ms Ingur's. Then, he placed her with the other frightened children in a specially made secret box in a warehouse he'd changed the locks on months earlier. He knew he was safe because he could derail Captain Estivan's investigation at any time by destroying evidence and that Mrs Dalur would do anything she could to help him maintain the façade until after she had left to go back to Corl."

"He's brilliant, isn't he?" Lija grinned and shook her mother's arm excitedly, blushing as he smiled back at her.

"You make it seem too simple," Captain Estivan grumbled. "It appears that it was an attempt to bring the underground slave trade to Mystentine. They were starting by making this a collection point, particularly for the people who were least likely to be missed by those in power."

"Did you interrogate the buffoons?" Wolflock asked.

"No. But we found instructions on their person. Apparently, Chestir was being paid to establish the operation here-"

"Can I see those?" Wolflock took a breath and held it as he placed his teacup down.

"Uh... it's not normal protocol to allow civilians to see evidence, but I haven't logged it yet so..."

Wolflock snatched it up and an awkward silence fell over the room as he read it.

E.

First shipment will not be delayed any longer. Setup of the Mystentine cell is taking too long. No more excuses. Twenty units and no less under fifteen. If there are less or spoiled goods you will make up the remainder. Any more mistakes and you'll be Sliced from the operation.

A.

Wolflock read it over and over, examining the paper, the cut edges, and the ink in immense detail.

"I'll need that back you know?" Captain Estivan coughed.

Wolflock scowled and quickly copied it into his journal. The texture of the paper, the style of ink, the handwriting, the punctuation, everything, he committed it all to memory and his book. His heart flared like a hot flame as he wrote. These people had not just abducted children, but they had treated them worse than livestock. They hadn't even been thought of as living beings, but as objects. Possessions. His chest burned with rage as he thought of how Mothy had grown up with this kind of treatment.

"Send word if you find anything," he growled through gritted teeth.

"Ha... sure, kid," Sergeant Estivan chuckled and put away the note in his file. "I'd best be going. I have to get these things back to the office and finish my report. I just wanted you boys to know that the city of Mystentine is incredibly grateful for your assistance. You've helped many families find their loved ones and we thank you for that. As a token of our thanks, the Guard of Mystentine wishes to pay for any expenses these lads need to get to the University tomorrow."

A grin split Wolflock's sore face, and he looked for Mothy, but his friend's face barely smiled and his eyes burned a dark brown. Was he as mad about the slavers as Wolflock had been?

"Thank you, Captain Estivan. That's very kind of you."

The captain nodded to Ms Vuori, who beamed and nodded to him, hugging Lija tightly to her side.

Officer Tand grinned, giving Wolflock and Mothy

a wink. "That was the most interesting case I've ever been on, and I hope it never happens again. I'll know that, if I ever see you two again, trouble is afoot." She moved to each of them and gave them a gentle hug. "Thanks for keeping Gretah a secret. Travel safe and merry part."

Wolflock tried not to smile too hard as his face still ached, but he waved Officer Tand goodbye.

"Merry meet again."

"Don't threaten me," she grinned and stepped out of the room.

Dr Växtadlare stayed for the rest of the day, monitoring Wolflock's health and making sure Lija was mentally healthy. Wolflock sensed a tension between the doctor and Mr Dalur, who lingered throughout the day. Mr Dalur couldn't seem to tell which room he was least wanted in.

The doctor insisted Wolflock remain sitting or lying for the day, and, as he stayed in the Vuori home, Wolflock had to obey. He'd hoped to speak with Mothy at some stage, but, as soon as he could, Mothy had said he wanted to explore the city and wasn't seen again until dinner started.

Wolflock spent his first waking hours writing to his sister, and, for the first time in months, a letter to his father. When he had finished, Lija approached him with a secret book she'd been compiling of the cases she'd taken from Captain Estivan's desk. When he asked her what the captain thought, she just grinned and blushed.

"Always better to ask forgiveness than permission. Most people don't know they want your help until after you've given it, anyway." He chuckled and helped her with the cases and how to look for the right clues.

Instead of conversing with Wolflock, Mothy spent dinner and supper expressing his gratitude for Ms Vuori preparing their gear, guide and the beasts of burden that would be pulling their luggage up the mountain.

When they sat around the circular table for dinner, it became apparent that Mothy had been regaling Lija with Wolflock's grand adventures and she was eager to hear more from the source. He entertained her and gave her some ideas of how to look out for future abductors when she went back to work for Captain Estivan. Mothy encouraged Wolflock to play them some music on his fiddle and the evening turned into a concert for Mr Dalur, Dr Växtadlare, Ms Vuori and Lija. Mothy stayed outside on the porch away from everyone.

As the flames in the hearth fire dimmed to embers and Lija fell asleep with her notebook in her hands and her head on Wolflock's arm, Mr Dalur approached them, and stroked his daughter's white hair.

"You were right."

"I normally am," Wolflock chuckled. "But, what was I right about this time?"

Uskoton sighed and spoke quietly.

"I did act selfishly. I thought I was going to make Ameiloe happy and free her spirit. But she doesn't want that. I've agreed to take her back to Corl and have our marriage annulled. If we strike it off the record entirely, she can wed a Troston man and, hopefully, live a happier life. Her devotion is so precious to her. By thinking I was freeing her, I took that away from her."

Wolflock nodded and stayed silent. Adult relationships were awkward and messy. Not something in which he was remotely interested.

"I'm sure you're wondering if I'm going to return to my relationship with Kiipei," the fickle man continued

Not really, Wolflock thought.

"I'm not sure she'll have me again, but I certainly hope so. It would be good for Lija."

Wolflock frowned and shook his head.

"You only think that because you want a family who loves you." Wolflock and Uskoton turned to see Mothy in the doorway. "Unless you're going to put in the work and effort needed to maintain those relationships, then don't even bother. Family isn't about you. It's about them. If you're not good for them, then don't engage as if you are. If you always work to be a good thing in their lives, that is when you deserve a place with them. Otherwise, leave them alone."

His strained smile quivered, then he turned on his heel and ran from the room.

They both stared after him and Wolflock rose to his feet. Something wasn't right.

Mr Dalur looked wounded by Mothy's words and raised his hand to his chest.

"That was a bit uncalled for."

"He's right, though. Children are impressionable. They're not for your own, egotistical whims. You either love them and do your absolute best for them, or you put someone in their lives that will." Wolflock didn't look back at the failed husband; he just knew he needed to be with his friend. "I'd best get to sleep. We have at least a two-day hike ahead of us."

Mr Dalur barely nodded as Wolflock followed Mothy up to their room. Mothy was already in bed and pretending to sleep, but Wolflock could see him shaking. Wolflock realised he knew very little of Mothy's father and perhaps Mr Dalur had reminded him of something terrible. He sat on Mothy's bed and put a hand on his shoulder, trying to comfort him the way his friend would comfort him.

"Your words affected him greatly. He should try to be a better father and partner now. I think Dr Växtadlare is a better option, though." After a few moments without a response he asked, "Are you well?"

His friend supplied no answer, but his shoulders relaxed as he let out a long-held breath.

"Sleep well, my friend. I'll see you in the morning. There's no one I'd rather make this journey with."

Wolflock didn't know what had changed Mothy's mood so dramatically, or what he could do to soothe it. He didn't know what the next two days would hold. He didn't know what trouble they would come across or how they would get through it.

He just knew that they were at the dawn of the final steps to the biggest journey in their lives so far.

Rhiannon D. Elton

Dear Myna,

        Mysterine is unglaublich. I kannen nicht glaube Baxta hennach getracht unt hir. Der zauber, der leute, der verangenheit! I has is. Mothy sagen I shas nicht scherzt zu ha während an shiet qual mehr intamet, aber I habe zu mitteilen ha sat I hennach etwel zu is. I hennach gekennt ha kannte et ein is sem ein statt. Der misenatur!

        I erzett einen Untrum mächen sem ein stals flangel, während gewahrenspurt ein sererxen seralten, uns beschlichen familshaft ausfragen, alle ein der tage. Ob sat is zur. Lashunt zagt sat. Fat. Zur tage. I bin retaunten.

        I bin abentet zu schlet shiet ein sem Mothy's lather.
Lather.

Dear Myna,

        Belflist hentene ther geschlet shiet lather ein, aber therm notexen sat zuu spaset nicht zu übermitteln. Ther is gut. Ther sat geschlet zag ein sererxnicht ther haben entselt aber wir habe einen retaunten erzten hir wer is aufsemet therm sehr gesunde. Ein hinge mehr zunde sen ruhe uns ther wixst er recht es wanan.

        Wir eins abentet hat der mexg zugemexgen, zu beduxnfit unt glut. I blib serder zu treffet ha uns Mexe felen gehnet ha kannte zu besughen.

Deinen Elebelich,

Mothy.

About the Author

Rhiannon is the walker between worlds. One foot in Earth, the other constantly stepping into Pelaia. As if gazing into a crystal ball, she sees this other world and all that happens within it with the clarity of someone staring through a veil. It is her purpose in life to transcribe these histories, adventures and mysteries for you to enjoy.

This witchy woman was raised by a fairy who taught her that there are all kinds of magic throughout the world. She taught Rhiannon to withhold judgement because you never truly know another's story. She also taught her that everyone, no matter how flawed, has something to give.

The adventures of Rhiannon's youth lead her through trials and dangers that taught her about the darkness within the world, but it also showed her that anything could be overcome. There was always a way. Surrounded by so much apathy and hopelessness, Rhiannon made it her goal in life to show others the light and that if they could dream it they could do it.

The way she was shown this was through stories.

Stories of friendship, love, adventure, discovery, compassion, understanding, and kindness. All of these stories gave her new friends, new lessons, new life.

In the depths of her darkest place during year 11 and 12, when she felt at her loneliest, drugs surrounded her life in terrible ways, the self worth of those she loved and admired crumbled, she was relentlessly bullied and felt friendless in her most trying years, she lived in squalor due to bureaucratic errors, and yet she still had to be "perfect". She had to perfectly excel in school, she had to perfectly remain calm and gentle in the face of abusive men, she had to be a perfect role model for all those around her. That craving for perfection in order to get love nearly killed her several times. In all of this darkness with politicians sacrificing real people and real environments for imaginary money, with teachers displaying no compassion for their students, with men abusing women and children, with communities vilifying those who needed them most, with injustice reigning and all hope seemingly lost... Puinteyle was born.

All of these pains in life were fixed in Puinteyle.

All of them were able to be mended and healed because of a conscientious effort. The people of Puinteyle wanted to be better than their problems. Puinteyle was where people made an effort to love freely and always sought to help each other, animals and the environment. Harmony. True and beautiful harmony. Where the pendulum never swayed too far away from that beautiful harmonious and happy point of balance.

But like in our lives, there is always obstacles to overcome and darkness to understand. Therefore, Puinteyle would always have its own inner turmoils to learn and grow from too. Thus, the stories never truly end.

Rhiannon has always lived and breathed stories, knowing her role in life is to be this guide through a new world for others. Her dream is to support her community with her stories, as well as creating a company where other artists can come together in celebration of Pelaia and all it has to offer.

Become Part of the Magic & Mystery...

www.patreon.com/RhiDElton

If you want more clues, more magic and more mystery, support me on Patreon.

You'll get exclusive clues, maps, sketches, behind the scenes stories, lore and much more! You'll also be the first to know when a new story is coming out so you can solve the mystery before your friends.

If you join at any tier above $10 you can get mugs, posters, bags and shirts, all with your favourite characters.

www.patreon.com/RhiDElton

Thank you for being part of the magic and supporting an independently published Australian author! Australia's independent authors need the support of their local community to continue to produce the books we all love.

If you enjoyed this book, please leave a positive review online (where you purchased the book or on Goodreads), recommend this book to your friends or family, or purchase another copy to gift to a loved one.

Stay tuned for the next mystery in the series:

THE WOLFLOCK CASES

BOOK 10

THE CASE OF THE MOUNTAIN'S MONSTER

www.rhiannoneltonauthor.com

 RhiDElton

 RhiannonEltonAuthor

 RhiDElton

 rhiannoneltonauthor

 Rhiannon D. Elton

 RhiDElton

THE WOLFLOCK CASES

1. The Case of the Captain's Hair

2. The Case of Mothy

3. The Case of the Curse of Houl

4. The Case of the Bitter Draught

5. The Study in Silver

6. The Case of the Lost Mermaid

7. The Case of the Pisces Moon

8. The Case of the Haematophagous Equine

9. The Case of the Lost Antrum

10.   The Case of the Mountain's Monster